I woke up at about two in the morning. My fingers, where The Claw had touched me, were hot and blistered and made my whole hand ache. Maybe The Claw had given me blood poisoning or gangrene.

Feeling very sorry for myself, I scrunched up on my bed in my clothes in the dark, longing for my Gran to come, call, do *something* about my hand and my mom and Brightner. I took out the silver glove and folded it under my cheek. It brought back very clearly the bristle-faced flea market vendor who had sold the glove to me, and the two women going through the box of shoes next to me and laughing about how out-of-style they were.

All of a sudden it hit me: tomorrow was *Saturday*. Flea Market Day. The glove had told me where to find my runaway Gran.

Other Bantam Starfire Books you will enjoy

The Silver Glove

Suzy McKee Charnas

BANTAM BOOKS

NEW YORK · TORONTO · LONDON · SYDNEY · AUCKLAND

RL 6, IL age 12 and up

THE SILVER GLOVE

A Bantam Book

PRINTING HISTORY
Bantam hardcover edition / March 1988
Bantam paperback edition / June 1989

The Starfire logo is a registered trademark of Bantam Books,
a division of Bantam Doubleday Dell Publishing Group, Inc.
Registered in U.S. Patent and Trademark Office and elsewhere.

Library of Congress Cataloging-in-Publication Data

Charnas, Suzy McKee.
  The silver glove.

  Summary: A New York City teenager teams up with
her sorceress grandmother to protect her mother
from her new boyfriend, an evil wizard bent on stealing
people's souls.
  [1. Fantasy.   2. Mothers and daughters—Fiction.
3. New York (N.Y.)—Fiction]   I. Title.
PZ7.C38193Si 1988   [Fic]   87-27092
ISBN 0-553-27853-3

Published simultaneously in the United States and Canada

Bantam Books are published by Bantam Books, a division of
Bantam Doubleday Dell Publishing Group, Inc. Its trademark,
consisting of the words "Bantam Books" and the portrayal of
a rooster, is Registered in U.S. Patent and Trademark Office
and in other countries. Marca Registrada. Bantam Books, 666 Fifth
Avenue, New York, New York 10103.

PRINTED IN THE UNITED STATES OF AMERICA

O   0 9 8 7 6 5 4 3 2 1

This book is for Nana.

Acknowledgments

Many thanks to everyone who read this for me—Jo, Steve, Robin, Bethinia, Lynn, Annette Schowers, Joan and Emily Gross, many others—and to my friends in the WPC as always.

Contents

The Silver Glove

1

Runaway

I knew something unusual was up when my mom came slamming in, later than she usually comes in from her office, her arms full of bundles and fire in her eye. "Valli, who in the *hell* have you been talking with on the phone? I've been trying to reach you for an hour and a half!"

I said a quick good-bye to Megan and followed Mom into her bedroom, trying to explain how I was only just helping Megan with a homework assignment she'd missed.

"You just saw the girl in school today, didn't you?" Mom yelled, dumping her load of stuff onto the bed. "I don't understand why you have to talk with her on the phone for hours afterward! I need to have this phone line open, Valli, in case— "

And to my horror, she flopped down on the bed and began to cry.

I was about to beat a retreat from the whole thing—

crying grown-ups are a major, unhandleable jolt for me—when I recognized some of the stuff on the bed. What I was looking at were the belongings of my grandmother, who had lived for several years in a rest home in New Jersey.

Gran's dead, I thought, going all splintery inside.

Mom looked up, wiping at smeared makeup with a tissue from the bed table. She must have read the thought on my face, and she quit crying with a gulp. "No, Valli, Gran's all right—I mean, she's *not* all right, but she will be all right, as soon as they find her."

"Find her?" I said stupidly. "How did they lose her?"

"Idiocy," Mom snapped. "She didn't come down to breakfast this morning, and when they went to her room, she was gone! I was out there in Jersey half the day. Nobody knows where she is, the police are out looking, I can't believe this—"

"But what are all her things doing here?" I said.

"I brought them all back with me from New Jersey, of course," Mom said, opening a suitcase full of Gran's shoes. "When she is found, I'm certainly not going to let her go back to a place where they don't have enough sense to keep an eye on a person with Alzheimer's! A person who might forget everything at any moment and do something crazy, like run away in the middle of the night!"

"Alzheimer's disease?" I said, completely confused. "But Gran doesn't have Alzheimer's disease."

Mom sighed. "Sit down, hon, we have to talk about this." She blotted her eyes on the bedspread. "I should have told you before, but I guess I kept hoping it wouldn't be true and I wouldn't have to."

So she told me now, and I didn't want to hear it any more than she wanted to say it.

"Mrs. Dermott called me from the retirement home last week. They did some routine testing of their residents last month, and Granny Gran—it seems she turns out to have symptoms of Alzheimer's disease."

"Not Gran!" I said.

2

Now, Gran did sometimes sort of forget who you were for a second, but she always knew when this was happening and she would start talking about shortcake, which was a private code she had developed to let you know that you needed to introduce yourself in some tactful fashion. But Alzheimer's? Never!

See, memory lapses to the contrary, my Gran was a special person, not just a regular old lady like most people's grandmothers. Lately my mom had taken to completely declining to even discuss Gran's special talents, so I didn't mention them now. Mom was upset enough already.

She went on, "The home isn't set up to handle Alzheimer's patients, and we can't take Gran in here, much as I'd like to—"

So then we had a long wrangle about what to do with Gran when she was found. Mom said we had no room and she couldn't be here all the time to look after Gran, and I said Gran could share my room and I would stay home and do my school by correspondence course, and Mom said I was sweet to offer but a girl needs her privacy and a normal education, and anyway, she had found a solution.

I could see that whatever this solution was, Mom was not very happy about it. "What?" I said. "What is it?"

"In a way we're lucky." She sighed, picking at the tufted knots on her bedspread. "The doctor who did the testing has a special research unit that studies people with Alzheimer's. He's offered to take Gran there. The cost is about what I've been paying the home in New Jersey, and Gran would still be within reach for visiting, though it is more of a trip."

Alarm bells went off in my head. "More of a trip? Where is this place?"

"In Buffalo."

"*Buffalo?*" I squawked. "Up there on the Canadian border almost, where it's freezing cold all winter? Mom, you can't let her go way up there!"

I knew how far it was. One summer when I was little I'd gone to a camp near Buffalo. I've never forgotten that endless, hot train-ride to a miserable place where there were leeches in the lake but they made you swim anyway. Those were the days when I was still a little kid, going by my baby-name of Tina instead of Val or Valli, but whatever name I remembered as being mine, those memories were horribly clear in my mind. I was truly shocked and upset at the idea of Gran going up there.

Which my mother picked up on, of course. "I'm looking into some other possibilities nearer to home," she said, "but nursing homes are so expensive! The Alzheimer's unit in Buffalo is probably the only realistic choice. God, Valli, this is all my fault!"

This seemed totally unreasonable to me, but typical of My Mom the Responsible One. I said, "How could it be your fault?"

"Someone must have told Gran about the clinic, and she thought I was shoving her into some horrible limbo in the back of beyond, that I didn't want her around anymore. So now she's wandering around alone out there somewhere, like some poor, deranged street-person—"

"I don't believe it," I said. "Mom, you shouldn't believe it, either—this stuff about Alzheimer's!" I took a deep breath and made the plunge: "Gran has talents, you know that. Special talents. She can't get Alzheimer's disease."

"Talents?" Mom blinked at me.

"Talents," I said. "You know. Magic."

"Valli, stop it!" Mom actually clapped her hands over her ears like a person in a soap opera who doesn't want to listen. Then she sat up straight and looked me grimly in the eye.

"Valli." She grabbed a fresh tissue and blew her nose. "Sweetheart, I know Gran is kind of special, I'm not denying it. But that's not what this is about. This is a plain, ordinary, awful problem about getting old and losing your grip, that's all. You've got to remember that and try to get through it with your feet on the ground. That's the way you can help

4

me get through it, too, and believe me, I need all the help I can get!"

"I *want* to help," I said. "You just turned down all my suggestions. So what am I supposed to do?"

She said, "For the moment what I need you to do is stay here in case there are any calls—especially from Gran herself."

"Where are you going?" I said.

"To talk to Kim Blaine about all this." Kim Blaine is Mom's lawyer, and also a good friend. "I've left Kim's number on the kitchen pad, if you need me for the next hour or so. If there's any news, anything at all, you call me there right away, okay? Meanwhile maybe you could sort through Gran's things and put them away for me. Use the extra shelves in the hall closet."

She hugged me hard, washed her face and slapped on some fresh makeup, and off she went to see Mrs. Blaine.

She probably thought handling Gran's stuff—actually registering that everything of Gran's had been left behind at the home—would convince me that Gran really was this helpless little old lady wandering around New Jersey with only the clothes she stood up in and no idea of what was going on. Huh. No chance.

There wasn't much to put away, really: a few faded cotton print dresses, old shoes all bulgy where Gran's corns had stretched them, two hat-boxes stacked full of hats covered with artificial flowers that she'd sewn on herself, little plastic zipper bags of nylons and slips and stuff.

Around six Mrs. Blaine's secretary called to tell me Mom wouldn't be home till after dinner. Mom had gone out to eat with Mrs. Blaine. I ate by myself, did some French homework, and remembered not to talk very long on the phone to any of my friends in case Mom called, or Gran.

The phone rang.

"Hi, lovie," said a voice I would know anywhere in a thousand years. Gran has never lost a little trace of the accent of Scotland, where she was born. "Something's rotten in Denmark, and I'm just off to find out what; so don't worry

5

your head about me. It's not so easy to nobble your old Gran, just you remember that! Did you get what I left for you?"

"No, what?" I said, clutching the phone receiver in a spasm of relief.

"Oh, goodness, don't tell me I forgot to—" she muttered irritably. "Yes, I did, here it is in my own coat pocket! There now, it's on its way. Keep it with you, you may well need it."

The mouthpiece got suddenly warm against my cheek. I jerked the receiver away from me and almost dropped the thing. Through the little holes of the speaker came this pale gray mist, hanging in the bedroom air like your breath on a cold day.

If you didn't know my Gran, you might have to be peeled off the ceiling over something like this. I knew her, and I was kind of jangled by it myself.

Before my eyes, the mist solidified into the fingers of a long, soft silver leather glove that I grabbed and drew slowly out till it lay limply in my palm. Then I heard Gran hang up, bam.

As I've said, my Gran had powers.

I recognized this particular glove right away. It came from the flea market they hold on Saturdays in the yard of a neighborhood school on Columbus Avenue. My mom and I sometimes go there to look for priceless antiques, which we hadn't found any of yet. I'd bought the glove for my Gran's birthday two years ago. Even though there was only the one glove (for the left hand), it was so long and soft and pretty that I'd wanted Gran to have it. Also, it was something I could afford on my allowance.

I put the glove in my pocket and went back to reading *The Count of Monte Cristo*, which was the only thing that could keep my mind off everything else.

Mom came in late. I sat with her while she had a glass of wine to calm her nerves before bed. I had already decided what kind of approach to take about Gran's call: the effort of not just blurting out the good news was fraying my brain. The trick was to present the news properly.

I said, "Mom, does Alzheimer's disease make you think people are after you? You know, make you paranoid?"

"I don't think so," Mom said, sipping her drink. "Don't you remember that program we saw on TV? God, I never thought it would come so close to home! Alzheimer's is forgetting, worse and worse forgetting, until you don't remember your own children or how to feed yourself. In the end your body forgets how to live and that's that."

This sounded pretty horrible, but Gran (thank goodness) was clearly in some other kind of danger. *Who* wasn't going to "nobble" her? "Does Gran have any enemies?" I asked casually.

"What do you mean?" Mom said. "How could a little old lady in a retirement home have enemies?"

"Um, well," I said, continuing my indirect approach, "it's not *impossible*, you know. What if she was a secret agent once, so secret that even you never knew about it; and now somebody's after her from back then."

To me, this didn't seem too bad for spur-of-the-moment.

Mom actually smiled a little. "Your grandmother was never anybody's secret agent. You see too many movies, my girl—*Granny Gran and the Temple of Doom*."

"I don't see as many as my friends do," I said. I couldn't even *talk* to some of the kids at school if I hadn't seen certain movies, but Mom has never been sympathetic about this.

True to form, even in the midst of her worries about Gran (one thing about mothers is how *predictable* they are about certain things), Mom said, "Let's not get off on that."

"Or maybe," I said, closing in on the forbidden subject, "it's something to do with, you know, Gran's, um, special talents."

Presto, Mom began to yell. "Look, Valentine, don't throw TV plots at me, all right? This is real life. Old people don't have enemies, and 'special talents' are not part of real problems! We live in the same world that everybody else does, dull as that may sometimes seem, and we have to cope like everybody else, too."

She sighed and looked at me sadly. She had big dark rings under her eyes. If only she would let me relieve her mind!

She said gently, "If you've got some idea that there's a dastardly plot to lock up Gran on the pretext that she's got Alzheimer's, please, please give it up. This is going to be tough enough as it is. I know it's a rotten deal, honey, believe me; this is my own mother we're talking about. I appreciate your sympathy and I know you're trying to help, but it's a matter of facing grim reality, not trying to sneak out from under it. Now I'm going to bed, and so are you, young lady. It's been some day. All we need is for one of us to come down with something from being overtired."

No choice but the direct one was left. I said, "Mom, wait. Gran's really all right, she told me—I spoke to her on the phone today."

"*What?*" said Mom. "What did she say? Where is she?"

"We never got around to that," I had to admit.

Mom jumped up and paced around the living room. "Valli, why didn't you tell me?"

"I'm trying to," I said. "The thing is, there's nothing wrong with her."

"Oh, a chat on the phone and you know more about her condition than the doctors do?" Mom flared. "So she was having a lucid period, that's all, it happens, but it doesn't mean anything!"

"Mom," I said. "It does mean something. I know you're not going to like this, but you have to listen. Whatever's going on, and she told me she wasn't sure what it was herself yet, it's something to do with magic."

"Magic." Mom put her wine glass down on the stereo and closed her eyes wearily. "No," she said. "It's something to do with a horrible disease that kills your brain, cell by cell. Valli, you've got to face it—"

8

"Look, Mom. She put this through the phone when I talked to her." I pulled out the glove.

"Oh, Val," she said, "come on. That must have been in with all the other stuff of hers that I just brought home."

"No," I said. "It wasn't."

Mom said firmly, "Then you must have picked it up in her room the last time you visited her at the home."

"Mom," I said, "you know Gran can do things."

Mom held out her hand. "Let me see that."

She took the glove and held it between two fingers as if it was poisonous. Then she whirled, opened the window behind her, and threw the glove out.

"Hey!" I yelped.

Mom banged the window shut. "Go to bed, Valli," she said. "NOW."

"Okay," I said. "Okay, okay."

Mom went into her bedroom and slammed the door. After a second, I heard her crying quietly behind it.

I tiptoed to the living room window and eased it open, hoping to spot the silver glove down in the courtyard for later retrieval. It wasn't there. It was hovering in the air outside the window, fingers spread. Floating.

I snatched the glove out of the air and rolled it up and stuffed it back into my pocket. *Then* I went to bed.

2
Brightner

The next morning I stayed in bed until I heard Mom leave, even though that meant I would have to rush like crazy to get to school on time. Mom didn't come and roust me out, either. One of the things that happened when she came around to calling me Val or Valli instead of Tina is that she began to insist on my being responsible for running more of my own life, which was actually not so bad.

The thing was, I really did not want to face her that morning. Her trying to throw away Gran's glove had been a pretty good indication that she was too upset to even talk to. I thought it wouldn't hurt to avoid more talk for a while.

In fact Mom had been moody and irritable a lot lately, ever since she'd quit her job at the magazine and turned herself into a literary agent. What with checkbook struggles and friendships changing and the hassles in getting used to the new people at the office where Mom now rented space, we had both been under a lot of extra strain before the problem of Gran's disappearance ever came up.

I had developed certain strategies for avoiding the worst of the fallout, one of them being hanging out in bed until Mom was gone instead of having breakfast with her. That's the one I used today.

So when I heard the locks click, I leaped out of bed and made record time for school, which turned out not to be necessary at all. We had an assembly first thing, which was welcome only because it was possible to slip in a little late, as I did that morning, in all the bustle and fuss of a whole school settling into the auditorium seats.

The assembly started out the same boring way they all do. To keep my mind off my troubles, I read more of *The Count of Monte Cristo,* the big, fat, unabridged edition which is good for weeks even if you are a fast reader.

My friend Barbara, who sat next to me, jogged my elbow to let me know that Mr. Rudd was getting set to launch. If he noticed you weren't paying attention, he tended to take it personally. Mr. Rudd proceeded to present the new school psychologist (the old one had married some kind of therapist and moved to California).

The replacement shrink made an entrance. He walked out of the wings and stood next to Rudd, looking down at us all. And right then I knew I was in for something, though I didn't have a clue as to what.

Mr. Rudd was an ordinary-sized person who wore dull clothes and bright-colored ties and a nervous, plastic smile to fool people into thinking he was dumb, which he was not. Nobody liked him much but he was okay, and he usually looked like a regular, boring, old grown-up person.

Usually. Next to this psychologist, whose name was Dr. Brightner, Mr. Rudd looked like a jerky little wooden puppet, a sort of bad try at Pinocchio.

Dr. Brightner was big, and sort of smooth and strong-looking. He had a thick paunch and broad shoulders, and he was a little bowlegged but stood very easily, as if he could move fast if he had to. He had a lump of a nose and jowls hanging over his collar and a pouty sort of mouth with a droopy lip. At first glance his face reminded me of Snoopy's.

Not the eyes, though. His eyes were small, bright, and quick. He kept his hands folded in front of him, and I had a funny feeling that he held them that way to keep the fingers from getting him in trouble by doing something clever and full of mischief while he wasn't looking.

"Well, boys and girls," he drawled in this husky, juicy voice, "here I am, take a good look. I'm older than some of your parents, and in some ways a lot more experienced. I come from a family of truckers, not a family of doctors or professors. In fact I used to be a cop."

That got him some buzzing all right.

He smiled, and it was amazing how wide and toothy that pursed-up, droopy mouth got. "Now you know the worst, right? It gets better. I didn't like being a cop, I got bored being a cop. So I went back to school to make myself into something else: a sort of minor-league shrink. My job is to be around when you need to talk to somebody besides the kid sitting next to you, somebody who hasn't spent his whole life in school. I've been outside, I know a few things. Try me."

My friend Barb jogged me again and whispered, "Better than old Matthews, anyway."

To tell the truth, Dr. Brightner did seem pretty okay. Interesting, at least. But this alarm kept dinging way back in my head someplace, warning me. Of something.

"I'm going to start out," he said, "by asking a few of you to come by my office and spend a little of your free time talking to me so I can get a feel for this place. I need to know the kinds of things that are on people's minds. And I'd like something to do until somebody flips out and really needs my attention."

He took a piece of yellow paper out of his pocket. "I've got a list here," he said, "which I will not read out loud. The people I've selected to be my first contacts on this planet—"

Laughs. "—will get a note from me in the next day or two, inviting them to drop by."

Clang. I knew I was going to be one of those kids.

Sure enough, after lunch I got a mimeographed slip delivered to me in French class. It read, "Please come to my office at _____ for a talk today. Brightner." He had filled in the hour that my free period started that afternoon.

Phooey, I thought; that's all I need, a friendly chat with a nosy stranger. I only had one thing on my mind, naturally, but you don't go and discuss your magic grandmother with anybody at school. I hadn't said anything to Barb, even.

My friend Lennie came drifting over as I left the classroom, and I put the summons in my pocket.

He said, "Hey, Val, could you do me a favor?"

"Sure, what?" I said.

He lowered his voice and moved a little closer to me, looking down at his shoes in embarrassment. "You know that thing I wrote for English? Petterick wants me to read it out loud to the class. I hate reading out loud. Could you read it for me?"

"Oh, come on," I said, "you're not *that* shy!"

He was, though. Lennie grew up with Spanish as his first language, and he had a little bit of an accent and would sometimes even stammer in English.

So I ended up reading his "Letters from Another World" (we were doing a unit on great travel-writing) for him in English. It was about some creatures called the wigpeople, and here's a sample: " 'They sent her home from work because she said she was a wigman or wigwoman. There had been quite a problem in these parts about the wigpeople, did I ever tell you? Huge, huge wigs wandering under the copper beeches, and, Mabel, you can just see the funny toes in the striped socks sticking out through the ends of the hair.' "

The reading got started late, but it was a huge success and it actually took my mind off Gran and Mom. I really got into it and started clowning around and leaving room for the laughter, and what with one thing and another, I only got through about half of it.

Everybody wanted me to read the rest on Monday, and Mr. Petterick said he'd schedule it in. Lennie made me promise him personally that I would do it.

It was all very exciting and gratifying, and it was the last real fun I was to have for what felt like forever.

Time for my appointment with the shrink.

He sat in the old, oak swivel chair with scars all over the wood. His desk, more scarred oak, was piled with file folders in different colors. He had a couple of magazines open in front of him, as if he'd been reading two articles simultaneously.

He was wearing a very sleek gray suit. I couldn't help noticing his socks, which were gray with an electric blue stripe down them, and his black, shiny shoes. This was no ordinary, shabby, poverty-stricken school staffer. I was impressed.

I sat down, put my bookbag on the floor, and braced myself for the usual exploratory questions. He smiled at me and asked me how I was spending the money that I had been stealing from my mother.

My jaw dropped, leaving me literally speechless for about a minute. That's a longer time than you'd think.

The thing was, he was right. Lately, just now and then, I would sneak a quarter or two, or maybe even a whole dollar, from my mom's purse before she got up in the morning. I would tell myself that *a,* it was payment for extra chores and *b,* as soon as I could I would pay it back anyway. Mostly I did my best to forget it each time it happened, which was not easy. I mean, my mom and I get along a lot better than most kids and their mothers, so why was I taking this stupid risk of spoiling it all?

Mind you, in third grade I went through nearly a year of telling the most outrageous lies, and then it stopped; and I never figured that one out, either. I guess it was just a phase, and maybe that's what this was, too.

14

Anyway, filching quarters was not what I had expected to discuss with this guy Brightner. For one thing, how the dickens did he even know about it?

Into the ringing silence in his office I said squeakily, "What money?"

"The money you take out of her wallet in the mornings before she wakes up."

"She told you that?" I said, playing outraged innocence over the pure panic I actually felt.

I was sure Mom hadn't said anything to this guy about my pilfering, because she didn't know about it herself. When my mother knows something about me that's bad and is supposed to be a secret, like that I've been to an all-night movie instead of sleeping over at Barb's or Megan's where I'm supposed to be, she gets this sad, tired look as if she's discovered I've been selling military secrets to Russia. She sits me down and starts to discuss my little deception very calmly and openly, and then we scream at each other for a while about different interpretations of the words "trust" and "privacy." In the end we work out some kind of return to normal.

There had been no such scene about missing money, though. Besides, Dr. Brightner was brand-new. There hadn't been *time* for Mom to talk to him.

But if she hadn't told him about the money, how did he know? My mind raced.

Dr. Brightner read it.

"No," he said. "She didn't tell me." He let me think about that for a minute. I was feeling pretty sweaty by then.

"Have some candy," he offered, leaning across the desk to shove a little plate of things that looked like tiny pink-, yellow-, and white-coated seeds at me. They smelled faintly like licorice. "You are kind of skinny for a girl your age. You're not one of these self-starvers, are you?"

I shook my head wordlessly.

"I'm glad to hear that." He sat back again comfortably

15

and quirked his eyebrows up. "Are you saving up the stolen money to run away, by any chance?"

"Runaways screw up their lives," I said with as much haughtiness as I could muster. "I'm not that dumb."

"Of course not," he said soothingly. "But you did run off once before. It's in your school record."

Well, I did once take a little time off for some urgent private business having to do with my grandmother and her magic. But nobody at school knew about that, and anyway, it was past and done with. What could it have to do with snitching change from Mom's purse now?

He let me think some more, which I did, sort of. We are talking good and scared here. I had to stop looking at Dr. Brightner because I had this awful feeling that he was reading my brain through my eyes.

I glanced around desperately. On his wall was a poster, framed: one of those meatloaf cats sitting on a stool and strumming a guitar. The words underneath—with notes to show that the cat was singing them—were about how he loved to eat "mousies."

I knew who today's mousie was.

Dr. Brightner said, in that same rich, velvety drawl, "Maybe you were trying to get to Alaska that time, to see your father?"

I said, "My *father*? What for?"

"Do you miss your father?" Now he was starting to sound like a shrink, which was comforting, in a way.

"I don't know," I said. "Not anymore. Not for a long time."

"Sure you won't have some candy?" he said. "Take two, they're small. No calories. No? Suit yourself." He grabbed the dish and popped a handful of the colored seeds into his own mouth. They crunched in his teeth. "A girl should have a father. Don't you think so, Tina?"

My name is Valentine, or Val for short, and I did not appreciate this guy using my baby-name that I don't use

16

anymore. It didn't seem worth the effort to make a fuss about it, though. I was in a lot more trouble than that here.

He went on, "I think you and I and some older member of your family need to sit down together and talk about what happened when your father left. Maybe someone who wasn't directly involved but who was around and remembers how it was. Someone who could help us straighten things out."

"What things?" I said.

"Oh, this and that." He cocked his head consideringly. "You could bring your grandmother to see me. You do have a grandmother? I'm sure she knows as much as anybody about your family history. In fact, I bet she knows more than most people do about most things. I'd really enjoy the opportunity to have a chat with her."

A quiver of irrational fear went through me. I mumbled, "I don't know where she is."

"Don't you?" he said. "You're sure?"

"Well, sure I'm sure! She was in a retirement home in New Jersey, but she ran away. Nobody knows where she is."

"That's a pity," he said. He went very still, which felt weirdly menacing. Black darts seemed to flash out of his eyes at me. I had trouble breathing, as if his black looks were poisoning the air.

I couldn't think. All I wanted to do was get out of there. I grabbed my books and gabbled something about having to go study for my next class.

He got up and walked around his desk and around me, and he opened his office door for me, very ceremoniously. "Of course; but you'll let me know if you hear from your grandmother, won't you?"

I sidled out past him, smelling the faint cloud of licorice that hung around him. All the way down the hall I could feel him gazing thoughtfully after me, and what he was thinking I didn't want to know.

What had I ever done to this guy?

The rest of the day ground along the way a school day does. I convinced myself after a while that nothing special had happened, that I was under a strain and had sort of freaked, that's all.

Still, I cut drama club—I'd had enough drama for one day, thanks—and went home fast instead of hanging around outside with my friends or going for a soda.

Mom wasn't there. She'd left a message on the answering machine for me.

"Valli, I'll be late for dinner. The school psychologist called and asked me to see him. I hope this isn't going to lead to a showdown between you and me, which is the last thing either of us needs right now. Don't forget to pick up the clothes at the cleaners."

Dr. Brightner wanted to talk to my mom? About what? The stealing, of course! Good grief, as if she didn't have enough on her mind already! I was stricken with guilt, not to mention sheer miserable embarrassment.

Maybe he would explain to her that lots of kids steal cash from their mothers at a certain stage. Maybe there was even a technical term for it among psychologists so they didn't have to lay it out to each other all over again every time they got together to talk about their victims behind their backs.

Or maybe he and Mom knew each other already, somehow, and she had in fact told him about the stealing and now that he'd met me, he wanted to make a report. There was nothing so terrible about that. Why did the whole thing make me feel so itchy?

Because my instincts are good, that's why, and in my heart I already knew that one way or another, this guy was bad, bad news.

3

The Claw

Through the window at Kress's Old-Fashioned Cleaning I could see that the place was empty. There was just the long bare counter across the back half of the room, and the winding rack of clothes hanging in their plastic sleeves, and the old-fashioned cash register with the curlicues on it in polished brass, and an open copy of *Vogue*.

Probably Mr. Kress was in back. He prided himself on doing all his cleaning and pressing on the premises. There were prints of old New York on the walls. He kept the lighting low and mellow, which meant you had to squint to see that the *Vogue* was five months out of date, or that he hadn't gotten the stain out of your skirt, or exactly what he was charging for not having gotten the stain out of your skirt. These days when I spilled something in my lap, it was a major economic crisis.

Mom was of the opinion that Mr. Kress kept a crew of illegal immigrants working in the back room under sweatshop conditions. This, she liked to point out (to me, not to Mr. Kress), would be the one really honestly old-fashioned aspect of his operation, the rest being pure, trendy hype. She said Kress's was an example of the galloping gentrification that was eating our neighborhood.

I felt grouchy and tired. I wished I was back in the noisy, plastic, fluorescent Eco-Wash Dry Cleaning Available on West 74th Street, where they farmed out your dry cleaning to some enormous central cleaning outfit and you took your chances on whether you'd ever see your clothes again. They had closed and opened up again as The Olde Salte Seller, a gourmet kitchen shop decked out like a ship-supply warehouse. So Kress's it was.

I opened the door and went inside.

"Mr. Kress?" I said.

No answer. The radio was playing very softly. And out of it came a voice that rooted me to the spot, as they say.

Dr. Brightner's ripe, rich tones said, "But you have to realize, Mrs. Marsh, that she's never really made her peace with her father's abandonment of you both."

GOD. I was hearing Dr. Brightner talking to my mom. About me.

I could not move. Air slipped in and out of my open mouth in skinny little sips.

"My concern is that without a male figure to anchor her at this crucial time in her life she's liable to cut and run. Not all runaways are abused children, you know. Some of them are sensitive kids reacting to rather ordinary situations they don't feel they can cope with."

Could they be having their meeting in the back room of the cleaners, for cripes' sake? And piping their conversation out front through Mr. Kress's stereo system? Was I just plain going crazy?

"Mr. Kress!" I screamed.

"There are all kinds of ways a kid can yell for help, you know," the radio continued. "I think Tina's sullenness and total lack of cooperation with me today was that kind of signal. I don't mean to scare you, but I think it's realistic to think of her as a potential runaway, given her history and her problems."

My problems! What problems? What kind of crap was he dishing out to my mom, anyway? He'd only seen me for ten minutes, for cripes' sake, and he'd done all the talking!

I had to get out of there.

I almost dislocated my arm, trying to yank the door open. It wouldn't budge. It was as solid as if it had been nailed shut.

And the big plate-glass window had changed. I couldn't see through it to the outside anymore. The glass had become a mirror, and in it, behind me, I saw something moving.

The mechanized clothes rack was turning all by itself. Not only turning. Advancing, coming closer to me.

No, I realized, that wasn't what was happening at all, of course not, it couldn't happen. The rack was trapped behind the long counter. What was happening was that I was walking backward, backing away from the mirror-window, toward the counter.

And the flap of the counter had silently raised itself, and as soon as I moved through that gap the chain of moving clothes was going to grab me up. I was going to get sandwiched in among the plastic-shrouded garments like just another empty dress on a hanger, and the rack would trundle me back into the darkness to someplace that didn't really exist, someplace I couldn't ever get home from.

That was why Dr. Brightner was talking about runaway kids to my mom. Because he knew I was about to disappear, just like Gran! Except, I reminded myself feverishly, he didn't have Gran, not if he'd been so hot to get me to bring her to him.

Why didn't I hear my mother's voice? There was only Brightner's, and in answer, a faint crackle of static. He *wanted* me to be scared. He wouldn't let me have the comfort of hearing Mom.

My legs walked backward another step. I couldn't look away from the mirror image of the moving rack behind me.

"Tell me something about you, Laura," the voice from the radio went on. "May I call you Laura? Kids aren't the whole world, even though it may seem that way sometimes. It's no crime to give ourselves a little attention now and again, you know. To tell the truth, in my line of work I get lonely for some grown-up company myself."

He was calling my mother by her first name, for Pete's sake—coming on to her, when he was supposed to be having a professional conference! On top of that, he wasn't even bothering about me anymore, he figured he had me nailed down already. I was outraged.

I opened my mouth and I croaked, "Gran! Help!"

The image of myself in the glass continued to wobble toward the counter at my back, which I could feel looming very close behind me. The metal hangers rattled softly, like teeth being gnashed in a hungry mouth.

But way inside my mind words formed themselves, faintly, as if from far away.

The words were, "Put on the silver glove."

Granny Gran's glove, still in my jeans pocket! I fumbled it out with clumsy hands: soft silvery leather, wrinkled and worn. How could this discarded old thing that I had once been babyish enough to give as a gift help me now?

I yanked it onto my left hand as my legs carried me into the gap in the counter. I felt the first brush of the circling clothes against my back.

Warmth from the glove flooded my whole body. My fingers unclenched.

In the mirror a glittering claw of silver wire reached out from the rack, rattling toward me, ready to snag me and yank me in among the hanging clothes.

Brightner's voice oiled along, ignoring all this completely, though I was sure he knew exactly what was happening here in Kress's Old-Fashioned Cleaning. "I wanted kids

22

of my own, of course, I come from a large family myself. But my ex-wife—"

I couldn't tear my gaze away from the mirror image that had me hypnotized. Risking the moment of blindness, I clapped both hands over my eyes, and that did it. I whirled around and with my gloved hand I grabbed the glittering, reaching claw, set my heels, and gave the hardest pull I could.

The radio let out a shriek that went through my head like a needle of ice.

The claw in the clothes rack was so hot—or so cold—that I could feel its wiry pincers burning my skin through the leather of the glove. I gritted my teeth and hung on, straining against what seemed like the weight of the whole rack, the whole back of the cleaners place, the whole world.

It all came loose so suddenly that I staggered.

Out from among the clothes flew something like a silver skeleton, but of some buglike creature that never lived on this earth. It was all bundled wire, with a lot of whirling, glittering, skinny limbs that ended in catching claws.

I slung it away from me as hard as I could, yelling with disgust and horror. It shot through the air, all huddled into a defensive, angular knot, and it hit the mirror with a shrieking jangle.

Suddenly I could see outside again: the street, the restaurant opposite, a guy walking by with an attaché case.

"What's the rush?" came this crabby voice behind me. I spun around.

Mr. Kress shuffled out of the back room looking very annoyed. "I'm coming," he said. "I heard you. All of New York heard you. You might try to have a little patience, young lady. I do all my own work, you know, the old-fashioned way, here on the premises."

He held out his hand for my cleaning ticket.

The radio played the theme from *The Sting,* and The Claw was nothing but a bunch of hangers lying all tangled up in a heap under the plate-glass window.

4

Trouble, Trouble, Trouble

I walked home in a daze with the clothes over my arm and the glove still on my hand. I let myself into the apartment and fell on my bed.

The glove was unmarked, except for a couple of dark spots where my tears of desperation had fallen on it. I took it off very carefully. Two of my fingers were red, as if singed, where I had gripped The Claw for that instant before I flung it away.

It had really happened.

After a while I took some aspirin from the medicine cabinet and downed a small drink from the open bottle of wine Mom kept in the fridge. Barb and I had once done some experimenting with various bottles of this and that from the liquor cabinet, so I knew it wouldn't take much.

Sure enough, I conked out in about three minutes and I slept for an hour. If I dreamed, I didn't remember what of, which was probably just as well.

When I woke up around dusk, I wandered through the apartment reliving those crazy moments at Kress's in my mind and repeating in a whisper what I could remember of the conversation I had heard over Mr. Kress's radio. Everything around me was comforting and familiar—the blistered plaster and paint around the steam pipe in my bathroom, the pencil marks on the bedroom door that marked the stages of my growth—but nothing could wipe out the memory of that voice.

Mom got home at seven-thirty and she looked spectacular. She was humming to herself when she came in the door, and her hair was sort of sweeping around and her eyes were big and glowing and all that stuff. I hadn't seen her look like that since she had floated around for a week over some math professor from City College. He was actually not bad, but it didn't last.

My mom and I had been having some tiffs about our respective love lives lately, if you can call mine that. Just to put what follows into perspective, let me lay out here a brief example of the kinds of conversations we'd been having. They went like this:

Mom: "I wish you wouldn't spend so much time with this boy Lennie. You're too young to be dating."

Me: "Who's dating? We were just hanging out together, that's all. What have you got against Lennie, anyway?"

Mom: "He just seems a little, um, I don't know, flaky to me. Dopey, even. You know. *Slow*."

Me: "He's not. Anyway, it's not exactly a heavy romance, Mom. We just happen to know each other from first grade, that's all."

Mom: "First grade was a long time ago. I know all your friends are starting to be interested in boys, Valli, but I hate to see you get too involved with any one person so early."

Some of my friends were way past "starting," but that wasn't the kind of comment that helped.

Me: "I thought you were worried about me being a 'late bloomer' "—that was Mom's approach whenever she thought

I was spending too much time by myself, reading—"I thought you wanted me to learn 'social skills.' "

Mom: "Social means with lots of other people, not just this one boy."

Me: "What's wrong with Lennie?"

Mom: "For one thing, he's got one continuous eyebrow. Don't you find it hard to trust a person who has one continuous eyebrow?"

This referred to the fact that Lennie's eyebrows almost met over his nose. *I* happened to think that the slightly loopy, werewolfish look this gave him was one of Lennie's more interesting features.

Me, counterattacking: "That's *nothing* compared to some people. Speaking of hair, what about that client of yours who wrote the book on horned toads? You could shave the backs of his hands and stuff a sofa with the cuttings."

My mom, being divorced and pretty and terrific, did some dating. Her glamorous though shaky new career as a literary agent had somehow led to an increase in this activity. "If this doesn't work, I'd better have somebody on hand to marry," she'd told me at least twice, only partly joking. It also led to her being more watchful and nervous about me. I had begun to wonder whether I was going to have to wait until *I* got divorced to do any real dating of my own.

Mom: "Valli, don't get offensive, please."

Me: "Well, what's *wrong* with one continuous eyebrow?"

Mom (after a brief pause): "When I was much younger and lived in Greenwich Village, there was a Turkish painter who was madly in love with me. He spent one evening chasing me around the kitchen table with a carving knife. And he had one eyebrow."

And so on.

Now, compare and contrast the foregoing with what took place when my mom came home on the evening of the attack of The Killer Claw.

"Hi, sweetie," she said. "Have you had dinner already?"

"Nope," I said. "What about you?"

She said vaguely, "Oh, I was talking . . . walking . . . window-shopping . . . I forgot about food, to tell the truth."

She opened the fridge door and stood there casing the shelves and humming. You would never think that this person had a missing Gran on her mind, which was very weird. I began to feel anxious.

"Window-shopping?" I said. "I thought you were having a conference with, uh, with somebody from my school." I could not, so help me, say his name.

"That's right, darling," she said.

Trouble, trouble, trouble. When she calls me "darling," she's on some other plane of existence where men are gallant and kids are darlings and life's a dream. This is kind of endearing in a grown person, but it's also a pain in the neck as long as it lasts, which usually isn't beyond the third date.

"As a matter of fact," she said, "I've been with a delight-ful male companion, and it's somebody you know already."

Well, of course at that point I knew, all right. Window-shopping! For what, a new Claw?

I tried ignorance anyway, on the off chance that I was wrong: "I know him?" I said. "From where?"

She brought out some cheese and ham and took a bite of each. "Can't you guess?" she said. "Valli, darling, why didn't you tell me that the new school psychologist is such a sweet, smart, caring man?"

"Because he isn't!" I yelped. "And he's got a face like a— like a bulldog!"

Mom looked hurt. "Since when have you thought that looks were everything?"

"He's too old for you," I said. "Come on, he is a lot older than you are, isn't he? He told us he was old, in assembly."

She blushed. It was awful. "Well, maybe he is—I didn't ask to see his birth certificate. I didn't know you were so conservative, Valli."

"I'm not, I'm just trying to tell you—you *can't*—how can you stand him? He's a *creep*!"

She flinched, which made me feel awful. But I was desperate,

She recovered her poise, though her voice got an edge on it as she went along. "Look, I know it's against the unwritten code for a mother to get involved with a staff member at her kid's school. But you'd better face it, love, and learn to live with the crushing embarrassment as best you can."

I was now more alarmed than ever. Mom only gets sarcastic with me when she's defending something really important to her. "What do you mean, involved?" I said.

"He seems like a very nice man," she said, and she got a plate and sat down to start some serious chomping. "He gave up a substantial chunk of his free time to me today."

"What did you talk about?" I said, remembering what I'd heard over the radio at Kress's. What would her version of that awful, smarmy conversation be?

"About you, of course, but lots of other things, too: life, and the state of the world, and publishing, and how hard it is to go into business for yourself. I told him a little about striking out on my own as a literary agent. He's had two books published, did you know that? They don't know how lucky they are at that smug little school to have a man of his caliber on their staff. For once I feel as if the price of sending you there is justified."

She was so caught up in all this that she had poured herself a glass of milk instead of her usual Perrier.

I said, "You're going to see him again?"

"As soon as possible." Then she gave me a long look, and she said, "You're really upset, aren't you? Look, darling, I'm as worried as you are about Gran, but for the first time I've found someone who seems to have a sense of what I've been going through. Besides you, of course."

"You talked to Brightner about Gran?" I said, feeling totally betrayed.

"Well, of course." Abstractedly she gulped down the milk and blotted her mouth on a dish towel. "Oh, didn't I tell you? I guess I forgot. What a strange coincidence—your Dr. Brightner turns out to be the same person whose letters I have in my desk offering to include Granny Gran in his Alzheimer's study up in Buffalo. I *thought* the name was familiar."

What a coincidence! But what could I say? That I'd listened to part of their conversation on Mr. Kress's radio while Brightner's Claw—that thing had to be his—tried to nab me and haul me off into never-never land? Well, you can imagine how that would go down. I could, too, so I didn't even try. But I was sure that if only I could get through to Mom I could save us all a load of grief.

I compromised. I said Brightner was a bully.

She said I was overreacting to his concern, and that he was actually a very thoughtful and warm person who was worried about me. He had told her so.

I said the coincidence was crazy.

She said, what coincidence?

I said the one she'd just mentioned, him being the "doctor" who was so anxious to ship Granny Gran off to Buffalo, for Pete's sake, and also being the new psychologist at *my* school in New York.

She said he was a very fine psychologist who was pursuing his interest in mental degeneration from two angles at once: on the one hand he worked with the aged who were losing their marbles, and on the other he was interested in the young who were just learning to use their marbles. Can you believe that? She must have gotten it straight from Brightner himself.

This was getting worse than nowhere, and the tips of my scorched fingers had begun to throb.

She said, "Valli, are you all right? You look flushed," and she touched my cheek with the back of her hand.

"I'm fine!" I yelled. "I'm dying, if you want to know!"

And I flung myself into my room and slammed the door. The phone rang, and I heard her settle down to a low-voiced conversation (it wouldn't be Gran, then). I stayed where I was with the light off and sort of drifted off to sleep.

I woke up at about two in the morning. My fingers, where The Claw had touched me, were hot and blistered and made my whole hand ache. Maybe The Claw had given me blood poisoning or gangrene.

Mom was asleep. I could sort of feel that in the stillness of the apartment. She was sleeping, and I was sick, but I wouldn't wake her up and worry her with my crazy fantasies, not me. Let her find me raving in the morning, or unconscious, swooned out. Too bad tomorrow was Saturday, not a school day I could miss due to Claw-poisoning death.

Feeling very sorry for myself, I scrunched up on my bed in my clothes in the dark, longing for my Gran to come, call, do *something* about my hand and my mom and Brightner. I took out the silver glove and folded it under my cheek. It brought back very clearly the bristle-faced flea market vendor who had sold the glove to me, and the two women going through the box of shoes next to me and laughing about how out-of-style they were.

All of a sudden it hit me: tomorrow was *Saturday*. Flea Market Day. The glove had told me where to find my runaway Gran.

5

Bad Character

I woke up early with my wounded hand wrapped in the silver glove, and my fingers didn't hurt anymore. Nothing was left of the blisters but two faint red marks.

Mom was still asleep. I left a note on the kitchen table saying I had to go to the museum to check out something as part of my schoolwork, and that I would be back for lunch, just so she wouldn't get all worried if I was out for a while.

The flea market didn't open till ten. I strolled on Broadway, the glove rolled up and tucked securely into my pocket. At exactly five after ten, I cut over to Columbus and trotted up to the south gateway into the schoolyard.

The day was chilly and overcast, but the vendors' tables were set up in rows as usual. I bought hot apple fritters at the gate and ate them out of a napkin, scorching my teeth when I bit into them.

I wandered up and down the aisles between the rows of

tables, looking at lamps made out of duck decoys and a whole array of chromium car-hood ornaments and old tin candy boxes selling for big bucks *without* any candy in them and tattered books and ashtrays in every possible shape and form including a Scotchman's head, in a green tam-o'-shanter, with the mouth open for ashes. Really gross and stupid, but some people will collect anything.

Gran was nowhere to be seen. There was no real crowd for her to get lost in, either. The vendors wandered around buying stuff from each other and chatting together. There was a comfortable confusion and a lot of bright color, and I felt terrible. Because of Mom, and Brightner, and most of all because of Gran. Where was she? She had to be there.

I stopped to look at some beautiful Oriental carpets that a young Arabic-looking guy had spread out on the cement. This was the exotic corner of the market, I thought, glancing at the African animals carved in ebony on the next table over.

On the other side of the rug display, a little woman with her face hidden in the upturned collar of her shapeless coat sat shuffling a deck of outsized cards. *Gypsy Fortune* read the cardboard sign propped on the wobbly card table in front of her.

The "gypsy" was talking to somebody while she shuffled her cards, and the somebody was a bum if ever I saw one: a bag lady, your typical street person with layers and layers of stained and ragged clothes, plastic rain boots with leg-warmers on over them, oily gray hair sticking out from under a navy watch cap, and an assortment of plastic shopping bags stuffed with unnameable objects.

What a pair. I quit my surreptitious staring at the gypsy and her weird client, if that was what the bag lady was, and I studied the carpets. I love those things. I sometimes think about being rich enough to buy dozens of them and hang them all over my room and roll them up for people to sit on, like inside a desert nomad's tent.

As I stood there dreaming luscious carpet dreams, a

creaky voice said, "Tell your fortune, young lady? The gypsy knows all."

I glanced over my shoulder at the hunched figure of the so-called gypsy. The bag lady had gone.

No harm in trying, I thought. I said, "Can you tell me where my grandmother is?"

"I should say so, lovie," she said, turning her collar down so I could see her face.

I gaped like an idiot. She was wrapped in a huge tweed overcoat and she had cowboy boots on and she was, of course, my Gran.

Weak-kneed with relief, I sat down on the folding chair across the table from her.

The smaller writing on the cardboard sign, which leaned precariously against a red glass with a candle in it, read, *pay me what you think it's worth.* The flame of the candle wobbled in the chilly breeze that blew through the chain-link fence around the schoolyard.

I said, "Gran! What are you doing here?"

"Reading fortunes, lovie. Want to try the cards?"

I whispered (by now business had picked up, and there were people all over the place), "Who was that?"

"Dirty Rose?" said Gran. "She's mad as a hatter, but she's not a bad person, and she does notice things."

"But where've you been?" I said, "you and—and Dirty Rose? Mom and I have been worried to death about you!"

She gave me a sly little grin. "I don't doubt it, but the free life agrees with me, don't you think?"

She did look better than the last time I'd seen her at the home. Her eyes were sharp, with none of that awful vagueness that meant she was about to say something about shortcake.

I leaned closer. "It's Brightner, isn't it? Him and this crap about Alzheimer's and Buffalo! You had to get away from him."

"In a way," she said, neatly shuffling her deck of fortune-telling cards. The cards were big and had complicated, faded

33

pictures on their faces. She *did* look like a gypsy, or some-body's idea of a gypsy anyway. She even had a bunch of gold chains and beads hanging around her neck. Bracelets rattled on her wrists as she worked the cards.

She handed me the deck. "Shuffle," she said, "and cut until they feel well mixed."

"My fingers are greasy from eating fritters," I said.

"The cards won't mind," Gran said.

I am a lousy shuffler even with ordinary-sized cards. Barbara and I used to play go fish and steal the old man's bundle. I never really got the hang of shuffling. These big cards were harder to handle than regular ones.

Gran patiently watched me struggling with them. "You're not concentrating," she said. "Valentine, what's really on your mind?"

"What's on my mind?" I yelped. "The Claw and the silver glove, and you're wandering around with some wild-eyed street person, and *Dr. Brightner is dating Mom!*"

"Better tell me the whole tale, then," Gran said briskly.

So out it all came at a gallop while I struggled with the cards. Granny Gran sat bent over her clasped hands, her pointy little chin on her knuckles, and studied me while I elaborated excitedly on all of the above.

When I finished she said, "That's our man, all right. A bad one, Val, as bad as they come. That's what I've been checking up on, at Sorcery Hall."

So that was where she'd been!

I knew a little about Sorcery Hall, from Gran and a friend of hers I'd met once. It was a combination club, college, and professional organization for sorcerers, and its members kept an eye on worlds like ours to try to help keep us out of magical-type trouble. When promising magical talent was spotted in people, a sort of scholarship was of-fered, very privately, so that they could be trained at Sorcery Hall to use their gifts.

Like Gran.

"They know who he is?" I said, elated. Now we were getting somewhere!

"They certainly do," she said. "He's a rogue wizard who was denied membership on grounds of bad character."

"What kind of bad character?" I said.

"Mainly necromancy, which means interfering with the dead for one's own purposes and profit. From what I can discover, Brightner has been out in the dark parts of the universe ever since, studying and practicing on his own. He's become quite a wicked and powerful black magician."

"Ugh," I said, not wanting to find out exactly how he could "interfere" with dead people.

Gran said, "Ready? Cut the pack into three piles. Then number the piles, one, two, and three."

I did what Gran said. She picked up pile number one and dealt out a row of cards, faces down, five across in front of her.

I said, "What does a—a necromancer want with us?"

"Well, it's my fault, in a way," Gran said regretfully. She pulled out the reading glasses she wore tucked into her clothes, suspended on a cord around her neck, and set them on her nose so she could peer through them at the cards. "Dr. Brightner has been shipping people from the home to his so-called clinic upstate. One old gentleman's daughter changed her mind about keeping him there and had him brought back to the home, just until she could make other arrangements. I noticed something about him.

"He was much vaguer than when he left, for one thing, but more importantly, he had no shadow."

"What!" I gaped at the cards she was turning up: the first one was a guy at a table loaded with odd objects, and it was labeled The Magician and it was upside down. "How could anybody go around without a shadow? I mean, when light hits you, you have to have a shadow, it's the laws of physics."

"Which is exactly how I began to suspect," Gran said grimly, "that this old gentleman had been got at by a rogue wizard; someone who could suspend or interrupt the ordinary laws of physics, and what's more, cast a glamour on the victims so that no one, themselves least of all, even notices! That didn't work on me, naturally. I can generally see what there is to see—or not to see, in this case—glamour or no glamour. Dr. Brightner hadn't planned on running up against someone like me. When he tried to scoop me up in his 'Alzheimer's' net, I slipped away to do some investigating.

"The worst is, I've seen others in the same plight since I've left the home—strangers, people on the street, shadowless and unfocused in mind, lost to some wicked spell!"

She turned up another row of cards: people with swords, all upside down, and a monster card labeled The Devil. I didn't like to look at them, but Gran studied them closely, frowning, as she went on.

"He's a very busy fellow, our Dr. Brightner. He has a whole network of clinics, and other operations too, designed to bring people to him. Especially discarded people that nobody would miss much, you see. Dirty Rose was just telling me about a certain shelter that's been started for the homeless here in the city. It's operated out of a restaurant, of all things; Brightner has a sense of humor, it seems. This is not always a recommendation. At any rate, street people who get fed there come back without their shadows."

"I thought you said nobody notices," I said, "because of the spell—the glamour."

"Most don't. Rose sees because she's got a touch of true sight, mad as she may be. And what she sees frightens her, as well it might! This man Brightner is the worst sort of black magician. He's raiding our ignorant and unsuspecting world for purposes of his own."

"But what good is taking people's shadows?" I said, trying to remember if I'd seen anybody without a shadow lately. Nobody came to mind.

Gran turned over another card and said angrily, half to herself, I think, "It will turn out to be some sort of slavery, you can count on it. He takes their shadows to serve as fetches when he wants them."

"What's a 'fetch'?"

"The shadows will be sent to fetch him the souls of the original owners, and the poor souls will have to come! What for, exactly, I can't tell yet, but the signs are clear: it's nothing good."

I was appalled and fascinated at the same time. "I thought only the Devil did that: souls, you know? He's *not*—"

"Oh, fiddle, of course not," Gran said irritably. "He's a thoroughly bad man, and a clever one."

"Then what does he want—well, souls for?"

"That's part of what I must find out," Gran said. "The sort of folk he's after—old people, street people—suggests that he's not interested in their bodies. Which might mean he has other bodies he means to lock their poor captive souls up in."

"Ugh," I said. "What kind of bodies?"

Gran grimaced. "Giant lobsters on Ganymede, for all I know. Where's your imagination?"

"Yuck," I said. "How could anybody do that, even to people he barely knows?"

Gran made an impatient sound. "I told you, he's a necromancer. That's the kind of thing they *do*."

"Well, somebody should stop him," I said.

"We'd better," Gran said, moving the cards around. "We must."

"We?" I sat back from the rows of colorful cards. "Wait a minute. You found out about all this in Sorcery Hall, right? Aren't all those wizards there going to do something about it?"

Gran sighed. "They're very busy at the moment, lovie, with something else: a war, a wizard war in another place and on a scale that simply dwarfs us and our concerns. Their resources are already stretched very thin. I'm afraid they have no time for a little skirmish here."

"Skirmish!" I objected. "But this is a terrible problem, you just said so. How can they ignore us because of some dumb war someplace? That's not fair!"

"No, but it's the way things are, so we'd best not sit here wringing our hands. We have our work cut out for us, that's the truth." She sighed again. "I wish I were younger. So much for the golden years."

I was too scared to protest anymore.

"Don't gape, child," Gran said, "the cause isn't lost. Not yet, anyway. They've done the best they could at Sorcery Hall. They've sent me home."

What could I say to that? Sure, they sent you, my tiny little old Gran, to fight horrible big Brightner? I said, "But he knows about us now, Gran! He tried to get me to bring you to him. And he made a grab at me, and now he's after Mom. He's already after us all!"

"Oh, yes," she said. "I'm afraid that's true, lovie. I'm sure that as soon as I gave him the slip he got nervous and checked up on me. Now that he knows I've a magic gift myself and that I trained in Sorcery Hall, he's hot on my trail. And yours and your poor mother's, of course. He's not sure how strong I am, so he'd like to get hold of you or your mother to use as an argument, you might say, against my interfering with his plans. So he's turned up at your school, and in your mother's life."

Oh, no. My mother the hostage. "What can we do?"

Gran closed her eyes for a minute and didn't move. Then she opened them again and turned over the last of the cards, which showed a tower being struck by lightning.

"That looks awful," I said.

Gran swept up the cards. "It is awful. Well, your job is to try to keep your mother out of Brightner's clutches. I'm going to go to this restaurant-shelter with Dirty Rose tonight, in the guise of a street person myself of course, and find out what's going on there. Collie's Kitchen, it's called. Odd name."

That would teach me to make up stories about Gran being a spy in her youth! I felt as if a mean-minded Fate had been listening to that conversation and had turned my own imagination against me.

"'Collie's Kitchen,'" I said angrily. "Sounds like a restaurant for dogs."

Gran said, "I'll phone you in the morning when I know a bit more about the place, and we'll decide what to do next."

I said, "But if you get held up or something—Gran, Brightner's working in my school! He'll *get* me! And Mom thinks he's wonderful. What can I *do*?"

She looked at me critically. "Keep your wits about you and hang on to the silver glove."

I had an inspiration. "I'll give the glove to Mom," I said. "It saved me. It'll protect her, too, won't it?"

Gran sighed. "I doubt it. She fights my magic, always has, so how could it help her? You keep the glove. It will work for you." She tapped the table top with the corner of her glasses for emphasis, before slipping them back down the front of her clothes. "Now let's pack up here and I'll be going. Where is Rose, do you see her?"

The day had turned cold. There were hardly any customers now, and some of the vendors were closing down their stalls. The rug vendor lugged a rolled-up carpet on his shoulder toward a battered van parked outside the yard.

I helped Gran turn the card table on its side and I started wrestling with the rusty catches that let the legs fold in along the inner edges. I was boiling with questions.

I said, "You can't go, not until you teach me how to use the glove. I don't know anything, really, about what it can do—"

Gran held up one hand to stop me. "Look!"

There was Brightner at one of the gates, talking with a young cop. He must have waited outside my building and followed me, figuring that sooner or later I would lead him to my Gran!

And, like a jerk, I had.

Another cop came strolling up to the opposite entrance.

The third gate, on Columbus Avenue, was jammed by two guys trying to get all their boxes of brassware out at once. Gran and I were sealed up inside a twelve-foot-high chain-link fence.

Brightner had been a cop himself. All he had to say was that Gran had run away from an old folks' home, addled and paranoid, and that I was a troubled teen.

He stepped past the pumpkins lined up on the pavement next to the jellies and the potted plants. He came toward us down the aisle between the tables, his hands in the pockets of his beautiful cashmere coat. I could see his toothy smile.

Granny Gran snatched me by the hand and dragged me onto the middle of the largest of the carpets, which still lay unrolled on the cement as flooring for the rest of the display.

Brightner burst into a run.

Gran pointed her finger at the center design in the carpet and muttered something that sounded like "Twelve o'clock high!" The carpet gave a lurch and shot straight into the sky, with me and Gran aboard.

6

Kite Fight

I shrieked a shriek they must have heard in Poughkeepsie. It was a short shriek, because the carpet went up like an express elevator in a skyscraper, the kind of elevator that leaves your stomach staggering around at ground level.

Past the edge of the carpet, which I was clutching with both hands, I saw the upturned face of Dr. Brightner. He stood with his legs braced apart and his hands on his hips, just looking up. Everybody else, including the rug vendor, danced around screaming and pointing up at us.

A cold wind from the west wafted us toward Central Park. The park looked like a carpet itself from that height, green and brown and full of random-looking sweeps of silver gray and black—cement walks and roadways—and blue plates of water at the reservoir and the lakes and the sailboat pond.

Gran sat in the middle of the rug with her legs crossed

and her hands folded in her lap, a little skinny genie in tweed and beads and those crazy cowboy boots. She looked awfully small and awfully old to be piloting a large flying carpet.

The thing must have been a full ten feet by twelve, all faded reds, black, and tawny gold. A thick beige fringe fluttered wildly at each of the narrow ends. I stayed hunched down low. After all, there were no guardrails.

"How are you keeping this thing up?" I said, running my palm over the rich surface of the carpet.

"I've woken the gift worked into the pattern."

"Can Brightner follow us?"

Gran chuckled. "This was the only carpet with the right design. I've had my eye on it all morning."

I said, "Let's go back and dive-bomb him! Can this thing shoot somehow, like a fighter plane?"

Gran said sharply, "Don't even think it! Power turned to destruction becomes a curse."

"That's not fair," I shouted into the wind. "Brightner gets to throw any old magical crap he likes at us, but we can't hit back? What good is power that you can't use to defend yourself?"

"If you want to counterattack," Gran said, "you must find a way to turn his aggression against him, which I'm afraid is beyond me at the moment, lovie. I'm half frozen and I can scarcely think and still steer this thing decently."

"I'm cold too," I admitted. "When can we go down?"

"I'm looking for a flat place to land," Gran said. "These are a bit tricky to handle if you're out of practice."

I didn't much like the idea of zooming around on a flying carpet with somebody who was out of practice.

We were right over Central Park now, and even colder: the sun had gone behind some clouds. At least we had company. In the sky were three kites, two above us and a smaller one below.

I had once spent some Saturdays in the Sheep Meadow with Mom, who had thought she might meet some interesting guy among the kite-flying enthusiasts who hung out there. I remembered getting an earache from running in the wind all day (I was pretty little then) and a crick in my neck from looking up.

I wondered if we looked like a giant kite from below. More like a manta ray, probably. The carpet was very slowly and subtly sort of flapping its wings: its outer sides rippled up and then down. This was certainly not the way magic carpets were supposed to fly according to the special-effects people who did these things in the movies. They always pulled the carpet flat through the air like something on rails, which I guess a flying carpet in a movie probably is.

This one was something else. I must say I found its ponderous way of flapping along reassuring. It made the carpet seem like an exotic animal with a brain of its own, maybe enough of one to keep us up even if Granny Gran got absentminded about the mechanics of flying the thing.

The smaller kite below us was a neat diamond shape, like an Oriental fighting kite.

I had made two kites and done a lot of research before Mom gave up on kite flying. In my reading I'd come across stories about kite fighting, which is a sport in Japan and Korea.

What they do is, they run a good length of the flying line, just under the bridle where you hitch it to the kite, through some paste. Then they roll that part in smashed glass and let it dry. When the line is taut, it's like a knife-edge that can cut other lines if it crosses them at the right angle.

The flyer who cuts the other guy's line gets to keep the downed kite as a trophy (usually the losing kite crashes and is ruined anyway). The kite is always small, so it maneuvers fast, like a hawk.

One of the larger kites above us, with a soaring bird painted on it, suddenly fluttered and jigged and began to spiral toward the ground. Its line trailed after it, cut down below.

"Hey," I said, "a kite fight!"

Well, sort of. You're only supposed to use a fighting kite against other fighting kites, of course. Cutting down ordinary kites is crude.

The little kite was no longer below us but darted above, heading across the line of the second big kite, a huge one painted with a snarling samurai face.

I peeked over the edge of the carpet, trying to see who was flying the kites. The meadow was scattered all over with the little dark figures of people strolling, throwing Frisbees, practicing karate and so on.

"A kite what?" Gran said distractedly. "Blast it, this light is so hard to see by. I don't want to bring us down in the trees!"

"That samurai kite's no fighter," I said. "It's not even the right shape. This little guy must be a pirate, chopping the others out of the sky for kicks."

The fighter kite was painted with a black and orange stripe design, like tiger fur, with a yellow cat's eye in the center. It was chasing the bigger kite, which floated lower.

Then the wind shifted and suddenly the two kites collided and dropped. The tiger kite shot free and the samurai kite just fell out of the sky, looking ragged and torn. The little fighter zigzagged high into the air directly above us, undamaged.

I couldn't help but admire the thing, with its wedge-shaped tail and the arched cross-strut that made it look like a bow-and-arrow drawn to fire. Too bad it was being flown by a bully.

A rasping noise made me look to my left. The flying line of the fighter kite was sawing at the edge of our carpet, tearing at the heavy wool fibers.

"Gran!" I yelled. I made a grab for the string, but the kite shot clear and the line was snatched out of my reach.

Our carpet trailed a wispy curl of thread where it had been frayed.

We both looked up.

44

The tiger kite floated above us, its painted eye looking blank and innocent. Innocent, for Pete's sake, what was I thinking? It was just paper, glue, a couple of sticks of wood, and some string!

It fluttered suddenly and sped across our path, and the line hit the carpet edge at another place.

"Help!" I yelled. "Gran, what's happening?"

"Brightner," she shouted. "Or one of his cohorts."

I could believe that, all right. I could believe anything about that awful man. How in the world could we get away from him? I ached with cold and hopelessness.

The rowboat lake was below us now. We had been maneuvered over water so that we couldn't land. The kite string curved away down a huge, impossible distance back to the Sheep Meadow.

"Grab the rug fringe and hang on," Gran said. She lay down beside me, her lumpy old hands twisted firmly into the thick fringe next to mine. The carpet shivered under us and we banked and headed west toward the river, traveling so fast that I could scarcely breathe.

Nothing spectacular, mind you, no loops or rolls or zigzags, but flat-out velocity into the west wind. The kite chased us, but its line held it back. It got smaller, falling behind, and my heart rate started to slow to mere overdrive.

Then the kite made a dive, looped back across its own string, and flew free, its cutting line trailing maybe twenty feet—cut by itself.

As the tiger kite sped toward us, I saw something that made me shut my eyes: a metallic glitter of the sun's sudden light along the wooden frame—the edges of razor blades, fixed to the wooden spars. Now I knew why the big samurai kite had gone down trailing raggedy flags. It had been sliced to death, not by a fighting kite but by a killer kite.

"Hold tight!" Gran screamed in my ear. Our carpet did a sudden sideslip and fast climb that almost made me whoops.

Something brushed my right hand like a feather of fire, and we sped upward at a steep angle.

I opened my eyes and saw a line of blood along my knuckles. Below us, the killer kite stalled, turned, and shot toward the carpet's underside. We dropped hard toward the ground, as if to knock the killer out of the air with our sheer weight.

The little kite turned belly-up and crossed underneath us, hitting us a light blow. A three-inch slice in the weave opened right next to my knee.

The tiger kite spiraled off at an angle, righted itself, and sailed in a high, wide, mocking loop over us. Our carpet flew heavily now, losing altitude over the dull, rippled sheen of the Hudson River.

My cut hand hurt. The pain sort of merged with the cold that ached in my clenched fingers.

The tiger kite peeled out of the sky like a fighter plane in an old movie.

"Aagh!" I screamed. "Get away!"

Then the gulls came: big, white, noisy birds in a riotous gang looping through the sky. They swarmed around the kite and pretended to ram it, sheering off at the last minute. They stalled and flipped and clowned, squawking and nipping at it with their ugly orange beaks, quarreling as if over a choice piece of edible garbage.

The kite sliced through the mob of birds, leaving two of them streaked with blood. I saw one flutter down silently and disappear into the river.

The gulls screamed and attacked. A wild melee filled the air with drifting feathers and scraps of paper. The sun glanced off white wings and darting eyes. Two more gulls tumbled down, crying.

Then the kite plummeted, pinwheeling, the gulls after it all the way. They burst outward in all directions over the water, yelling and swooping to snatch bits of paper from each other's beaks. The kite sank.

One by one, the gulls settled on the river. The water lifted them in a peaceful, bobbing motion. They dug their beaks into their feathers, rooting around disgustingly for bugs to eat. I loved them.

"I thought they'd never come," Gran said. "Someone must have been feeding them over at the yacht basin."

I was shaking all over. "What *was* it? The kite, I mean."

"It was what you called The Claw," she said, "in one of its many manifestations. Basically, it's a sort of evil impulse that Brightner can project out of himself and into objects like that little kite, to animate them and send them to do his will. Like the hangers at Kress's that he organized into a monster, and now this kite—brilliantly done, too. I'd rather not have used those old friends against that, but I couldn't see an alternative."

"Friends?" I squinted to make out the gulls, pale spots riding the dark water.

"They're just birds, lovie, not spirits. I know how to get on their frequency, that's all. I wish I hadn't had to. They've a tough enough life as it is."

"Can we go down now?" I said. My hands felt like two bundles of icy cramps and my ears ached from the wind.

"We have no choice," Gran said.

We were flying very low, heading southeast, limping in off the river onto the west shoreline of Manhattan Island. We hopped over the West Side Drive, skimmed a parapet wall, and bounced in the air, just missing a big skylight of dirty, frosted panes. We landed with a bump in the middle of a rooftop.

I staggered upright and stepped off the wounded carpet.

We were on some kind of industrial roof with a row of skylights marching down the middle of it. The building—it looked like a warehouse—seemed to take up one whole end of a block. It was surrounded by streets on three sides. The fourth side was bounded by a narrow alley and a neighboring building. An old iron fire escape led down over the farther parapet into the alley.

Gran stooped and grabbed one edge of the carpet. "Come on, lovie, give me a hand with this."

To my surprise the carpet was very light and easy to handle. It folded not only in half but in quarters and then again, and again, each time getting smaller and less bulky. In no time we were standing nose to nose and Gran was smoothing down something that looked like a handkerchief. She tucked it carefully into the baggy side-pocket of her tweed coat.

"Poor wounded carpet," I said. "Can you fix it?"

"Oh, I think so," Gran said, frowning absently.

"He tried to kill us!" I said, shivering, and then I blushed to have said something so stupid. I mean, this guy was stealing people's souls. Trying to kill me and my Gran would be like swatting flies to a person like that.

Gran kindly ignored my foolishness completely. "Let's get cracking, lovie, before he locates us again." She set off down the roof toward the fire escape. "I must find Dirty Rose for our dinner at Collie's Kitchen. As for your mother, try to keep her out of Brightner's company." She looked hard at me. "This meeting they've already had—tell me, lovie, did you notice? Does your mother still have her shadow?"

"I think so," I said, trying to remember. It's not as easy as you'd think, recalling whether a person has a shadow or not. I mean, it's not the kind of thing you look for.

"I imagine she does," Gran said in a worried tone. "I'm very much afraid that he's preparing something special for your mother."

"What do you mean?" I said. "I thought you said she's just somebody to use as a sort of hostage, to keep you from getting in his way."

Gran gave me a thoughtful look. "And people sometimes let hostages go, when there's no more reason to hold them; is that what you're thinking?"

I couldn't exactly bring myself to say what I was thinking, which was that maybe we should let Brightner take his load of shadows with him, if only he would leave my mom behind. How could we fight him, just Gran and me? We had

48

just barely escaped alive, thanks to a bunch of greedy, rowdy sea gulls!

Gran leaned against the parapet. An ambulance went wailing by someplace way below in the streets. She said in a quiet, matter-of-fact tone, "Brightner is clearly willing to try to simply kill me outright, and you, too. So he doesn't need your mother as a hostage, does he? He must be interested in Laura in her own right."

"You mean, really? As a—as a date? As a girlfriend?"

Gran said, "We must keep her from him, lovie."

I groaned. "Gran, *she's* the mommie, *I'm* the kid. She's supposed to fuss about the people I go out with, not the other way around!"

"Do your best," Gran said.

It sounded completely screwy to me. I said, "If he's such a hotshot wizard, he could go out with anybody he wanted. I mean, Mom is pretty and smart and everything, but she's no movie star. What's the attraction for somebody like him?"

"Her share of the family talent," Gran said patiently. "Her unused potential. He's ambitious, he wants to pull off a real coup here, and evil magic is limited, you know. It's based on fear, after all, and lies. Your mother, now, has her share of our family gift, and captured good magic can extend the range of bad magic quite considerably."

"Wait, now, wait," I objected. "Mom has no power, she has no magic. She won't even *talk* about magic!"

Gran sighed. "I know she won't, but she is my daughter. She does have—capacities. The problem is, she's always ducked the whole subject. You know how the children of hippies end up becoming stockbrokers? Which doesn't mean that her gift is wiped out, only that she neither uses it nor protects it. So her unused magic is up for grabs, and that attracts a man like Brightner."

"Can't she see that?" I shook my head miserably. "How can she even *stand* him?"

"She doesn't know what she's dealing with," Gran said grimly.

I said, "You said he works with fear. So why isn't Mom afraid of him? I am."

Gran shook her head. "It's her own fears that he uses to draw her to him—fear of being left all alone, of being unloved."

"What?" I said. "But I'm there, and I love her!"

Gran patted my hair with one gnarly hand. "Of course you love her, but you have your own life, Val. She wants what a woman is supposed to want, a man in her life. And she's at a touchy stage right now, you know that—striking out on her own and all. Life's not easy for a divorcée with a child, lovie. She's still hoping for a knight in shining armor, I'm sure, like most women in her position."

"She goes out with a lot of guys," I said, picking at the bubbles in the tar on the parapet. "She should have more sense by now."

Gran said, "So she should, but obviously her vision's not too clear on this point. Well, it's partly my fault, I'm sure. Magic doesn't make one the perfect mother, alas. I made a mistake. For the longest time I didn't tell her anything about the family talent. I didn't explain anything. I wanted her to learn about life without it. She did, and she liked being 'normal.' And I grant you, without a smidgin of magic she went out and got exactly what she wanted—nice, normal, hectic New York rat race, nice, normal divorce, and no simple *sense*."

"She does okay," I said. I mean, Mom's not always easy to get along with, but she's not a jerk.

"I'm glad you speak up for her," Gran said, "but you can see as well as I can that 'okay' is not good enough when you are a sorcerer's child. No amount of normality can cancel that."

"I still don't see why he's after her," I said stubbornly. I really just wanted Gran to say that he wasn't, I think. And I wanted to keep Gran there, talking about magic on a warehouse rooftop, so that she wouldn't be gone on her undercover mission, leaving me alone.

50

Gran frowned. "I'm not sure," she admitted, "but it is possible, lovie, that he's expanded his plans from a minor foray into a major soul-stealing expedition on the basis of being able to use your mother's unrealized power himself. Building on her capacities, he could tear away a really great mass of souls to steal. He could make poor Laura his springboard to a triumph."

I looked over the edge of the roof. The rusted metal steps seemed to descend into a slice of absolute darkness.

"But you're not sure," I insisted. "You can't be sure that's what he's doing!"

"No," said Gran, "but I'm going to find out. I'm just trying to prepare you, lovie. This could be a dreadful business, more dreadful even than it's been so far."

I had nothing to say to that. I just wanted to cry.

Gran said thoughtfully, "Now, if by chance I do *not* get in touch with you in the morning, you are on no account to try to come after me. Whatever Collie's Kitchen is, it's no place for you. You can do more if you stick by your mother."

The idea of not hearing from Gran, for whatever reason, froze my blood.

She went on, "And one more thing: I wouldn't say anything about today, about seeing me—and especially about my plans for tonight—to your mother."

"Why not?" I said, stunned. "She'll be so glad to know you're all right, how could I not mention it?"

"Anything you tell her may get back to Brightner, and the less he knows, the better. You go down first, I'm slower than you are."

So I went down the fire escape first, trying to get used to the idea of my mom as a kind of double agent against Gran and me, and herself, for Pete's sake, and not even knowing it! That made me really hate Brightner, for messing around with my mother's mind so that she couldn't even be trusted with knowing that Gran was all right.

How in the world was I going to keep all this from just bursting out of me, anyway?

On the bottom landing of the fire escape I had to heave the last ladder free and let it down to the sidewalk. It was almost rusted solidly to the frame of the landing, but as I jerked at it to free it, it gave suddenly and slid down with an echoing crash.

I stood there a minute at the head of the last ladder, steadying my wobbly knees. I mean, what if Brightner was waiting down there for us? But there was nowhere else to go, so down I went with my back to the alley, rust flaking off the iron rails under my hands.

As soon as I stepped off the bottom rung, a voice said, "Hold it right there, kid. Put your hands over your head and face the wall."

Brightner's cops!

When I looked up the ladder, Gran was gone. There was just a grubby handkerchief patterned like an Oriental carpet, tied to the rail and fluttering lightly in the breeze.

7

Mom in Love

They were not Brightner's men after all. They were two ordinary cops who had been passing in their patrol car and heard the bottom ladder crash down.

I begged them to let me go and get "my Gran's handkerchief," and one of them shrugged and got it for me. Then they took me in, as they say, and frankly that suited me. That part of town is not someplace you want to stroll in by yourself on a weekend, when there's hardly anybody around. So I ended up at a police station on the lower West Side, telling a story about wandering around in a state of gloom and confusion over the disappearance of my grandmother, looking for her. I said I'd noticed the handkerchief tied to the rail, a handkerchief (I said) that had looked like one of my Gran's. So naturally I had pulled down the fire escape ladder to get to the bit of cloth, which I took out of my pocket and showed to the police.

And I held my breath, too, while they looked at it.

Suppose they—or I, for that matter—accidentally triggered its magic and it turned itself back into a flying carpet on the spot?

It just lay limp, however, and I tucked it back safely into my pocket.

So that was my story—your basic lame, limping lie, and they probably didn't believe me, but what the heck. The warehouse hadn't been broken into, after all. In the end they called my mom and she came and got me.

The first thing I checked for was did she have a shadow. She did. Sigh of relief.

Now, this is my mom I'm talking about, New York's most law-abiding citizen, who could not be expected to appreciate her only daughter getting picked up by the cops. She came breezing in, signed some papers, explained that I was a good kid but definitely under pressure about my grandmother, and yes, she would get me some counseling, and off we went in a taxi.

She hummed to herself the whole way home. The only thing she said was, "I hope this is the climax of whatever's going on with you, Valli, not merely the beginning."

And there wasn't a thing I could tell her, not without her reporting it to Brightner the next time she saw him. So it was just as well that she didn't ask me any questions. Weird, but just as well.

Weird because it made me feel as if I'd climbed into a cab with a nice but totally strange person. I mean, your mother is the one who *always* asks you questions.

When we got home, she sent me to take a bath while she made us something to eat. When you have a working mom, you tend to do all your socializing together over the dinner table. Which probably meant I'd get the questions with my food. I was not looking forward to this.

Though to tell the truth, Mom did not seem to be at all upset. You would think she picked me up at the police station a couple of times a week.

I came into the kitchen in my bathrobe and started

etting the table one-handed. Mom said, "What's wrong with our hand?" I showed her the cut the kite had made, not rying to explain it or anything. "So that's what they mean vhen they say a kid has been in a 'scrape,'" she said. "Better o put some Mercurochrome on it."

And that was that.

My blistered fingers were fine now, but the slice across he knuckles of my other hand had puffed up and turned ed. Brightner had gotten me again, the monster! I would ave put the silver glove on to see if that would make it etter, but I was afraid Mom would try to take the glove way from me again if she saw it.

When I got back from the bathroom with a Band-Aid on ny hand, Mom had put a record on the phonograph—"Vienna Waltzes," one of her more sentimental favorites—and was umming to herself at the stove.

It looked as if there would not be any questions after all.

"Heard anything about Gran?" I said, just to see what he would answer.

"No, darling, not a word, not yet." For a minute she ooked at me with terrible anxiety, and she was my own, ;ood mom, the one who was being stolen away by this evil vizard. Then she turned back to the stove, singing along with Strauss like someone without a care in the world.

A new and dangerous idea popped into my head. She iad to be looking forward to an evening out with somebody.

But she was wearing jeans and her country weekend xfords from L. L. Bean and a plaid cotton flannel shirt with ı wool vest over it. This was not how she usually dressed to ;o to a movie with a doctor or an author. On the other hand, ier eyes were made up to slay.

I began to get this squirmy feeling in my stomach.

I didn't say anything at all while she stirred the pot and squeezed in some lemon juice and loosened up the ground Parmesan cheese that had caked up in the jar in the fridge. I sat down at the table like a limp noodle myself, feeling spacey and miserable.

"Presto, pasta!" Mom cried at last, dumping out the pot into the colander in the sink. Then, olive oil bottle in hand, she went all serious again.

"Valli," she said. "I'm sorry. You're worried about Gran, aren't you?"

I had begun to wonder if she and I actually inhabited the same plane of existence anymore. With some relief, I nodded.

"So am I, darling," she went on, "but a person can't go around torturing herself all the time. It's not healthy and it doesn't help anything. So I've decreed a little diversion for myself."

"What kind of a diversion?" I said.

Mom was lifting noodles out of the colander with a red plastic spoon that had square teeth around the edges, kind of like a claw. I looked away; I couldn't watch.

"This may come as a shock, darling, but I'm going out. On a date."

"Who with?" I said. Bam, bam, bam, went my blood. Who else?

"Oh, you don't know him," she said lightly.

She was lying to me. Knowing I couldn't stand the man, she was lying to avoid an argument. I'd done it myself often enough to recognize the symptoms.

"Where's this guy taking you, dressed like that?" I said. "The Village?"

I could follow them, I was thinking, and protect her. Try to protect her, or something, but how? I kept wanting to cry, and wondering if Mom would notice if I did.

"He's taking me ice-skating," Mom said.

There was this awful disconnection from what was really going on. I mean, my mom is not a flake. She would not go out on a date with anybody while her own mother, my Gran, was missing! Only if the Master of The Claw, Brightner the Creep, had put a spell on her.

And Gran had charged me with keeping Mom away from him. How? I said, "We haven't gone ice-skating in years." Which was true. Mom took me a couple of times when I was younger, and then she lost interest.

"As a matter of fact," she said, sitting down to eat with a sigh of satisfaction, "your father, may he freeze his little hairy earlobes off in Alaska or wherever the hell he is now, courted me on the ice of the Wollman Memorial Skating Rink in Central Park."

"He did?" I was feeling really peculiar. There was no way that I could make my end of this conversation intelligent.

"Yes," she said, helping herself to sauce and offering me the ladle. "If I am a little old to be the mother of a young teen, it's because I was slow to marry, Valli, slow and careful. After all, I had the horrible example of your Gran and Malcolm to learn from."

What a time for stories about Grampa Malcolm! Or rather *the* story about Grampa Malcolm, the baker.

Gran had been sent here from Scotland by her family to marry him, which she had done at a very young age. He had turned out to be the world's laziest living human, and one fine day she had simply sent him packing. Eventually, after showing up occasionally at family gatherings for a few more years, he had retired to Florida and the family had lost track of him. Period.

I am going crazy, I thought, because I am too tired to stay sane. And my mother has chosen this time to tell me the story of her life because she is under a spell that won't let her see anything real that's around her right now.

"So," Mom said nostalgically, "there I was in my late twenties, beginning to think about the virtues of being single all my life and teaching English, when along came Jonathan Covington Marsh, your esteemed (at the time, because love is blind) father. He was a rising young commercial artist in a very successful advertising art studio.

"He had no money, though—he was paying off debts left by his worthless drunk of a father, clearing the family name by interminably emptying his own pockets. 'Draining the Marsh,' we used to call it. But we had a wonderful time

57

together on next to nothing. In those days, you could still do that in New York."

She smiled. I squirmed. She poured some low-calorie dressing on the salad—another sure sign that she's interested in somebody and therefore more than usually fierce about her diet.

"One way of spending a cheap evening together in the winter was to bundle up and go skating after work. You'd pay your fifty cents per person, check your street shoes, and put on your skates in the big main room.

"I remember how it smelled in there—of wet wool, mostly—and how friendly it all was. I don't know how many times I had to borrow a skate hook from some stranger to pull my laces tight. Valli, you're not eating."

"I'm not hungry," I said. I wasn't. She put salad on my plate anyway, and I watched the dressing leak out and contaminate the noodles while Mom warbled on.

"They played corny tunes through loudspeakers. We'd totter out on the ice together, laughing and staggering, and plunge right into this big, happy wheel of people turning to the music."

She sat back, dreamy-eyed. Her voice was low and sort of thrilling.

"Sounds cold," I said.

"It was cold. It was wonderful. You got proud of being good enough to keep from running into people who fell down in front of you. One place on the ice was blocked off with sawhorses, where the serious skaters did their figure-skating practice and their lessons. Or was it traffic cones they used to mark off the magic circle?"

"More spaghetti?" I said. Maybe I could get her to eat so much that she'd be too stuffed to go skating.

"I'm fine," she said, twirling some noodles absently on her fork and not bothering to put them in her mouth. "When we got hungry, we'd leave the ice and crowd into the pizza bar. I think it was fifteen cents a slice, and a dime for a Coke. Huh."

She laughed so happily that I just couldn't stand it anymore. My control snapped and I said, "Wollman Rink is closed. More leaks in the pipes under the ice, it said in the paper."

Wollman had developed its first problem since they had renovated it. This was not big news anymore. But Mom looked as if I'd slapped her. "And that makes you happy, right? Damn it, Valli, why are you being such a *bitch*?"

Tears glittered in her eyes. I stared down at my heaped plate. "So where is he going to take you skating?" I insisted. I had to know. Couldn't she sense how desperate I was?

She said, "What is it, you can't stand the idea of your rotten old mom ever having had a good time in her life, let alone possibly getting to have a good time again for a change?"

I'm losing, I thought. I said, "You always want to know where I am when I go out, even with just Barb or Megan, for Pete's sake!"

"The situation is not exactly the same," Mom said icily. She shoved her chair back from the table.

I got up and went to scrape the food off my plate into the garbage. It was making me feel queasy just to look at the stuff. "So when is—this guy coming to pick you up?"

"He isn't," she said. "I'm meeting him."

All I could say was, "Don't go, Mom."

"Hey," she said, "I was born and raised in this town. I can take care of myself."

"Don't go." I felt about two years old.

She groaned dramatically, got up, and came over to hug me. "Come on, Val, lighten up. Give your old mom a break. God knows she needs one."

I grabbed at her hand, but there was this pain in my knuckles and I couldn't close my fingers.

Mom didn't seem to notice. She went waltzing off to the hall closet. "Leave the dishes, darling, if you've got too much homework."

I heard her but I wasn't listening. I was suddenly dizzy

and light-headed, and everything seemed far away and slowed down.

The front door slammed.

I ran out after her. She wasn't even waiting for the elevator, she was so eager. I said, "Mom!" Halfway down the top flight of stairs, she stopped and looked up at me.

She'd put on a dark blue ski jacket she'd bought once to go on a "ski weekend." She'd told me later how the first time she got on a beginners' slope and bent over to fumble around with the bindings of her rented boots, a single ski whizzed down from someplace above her at about forty miles an hour and shot past an inch from her nose. That was that: a broken leg was a reasonable risk to run, but not a runaway ski jammed through your head. She never went again.

The jacket looked great.

"If there's any message about Gran, write it down for me, okay?" she said. "Remember, don't stay up too late. 'Bye, Valli."

She turned and ran down the stairs singing the "Blue Danube" waltz or maybe the one called "Tales from the Vienna Woods," I always get those two mixed up. It hurt me a lot to see her look so happy and young, and to know she was heading for disaster.

My right hand felt on fire and twice its real size, and the stairs wavered in front of my eyes. I remember thinking, "I'm sorry, Gran," over and over as I wobbled around in a little circle in the hall. I'd had my chance and I'd failed.

All I could do was to stumble back to the living room couch and fall down on it, where I either slept or passed out.

When I woke up, sunlight was pouring in the windows. My hand felt okay. The cut had scabbed over. My clothes weren't even wrinkled, as if I hadn't moved all night once I'd corked off.

The apartment felt empty: sunny, still, and void.

8

Me in Shock

From her bedroom doorway I could see that Mom was there, all right, curled up under the big red quilt with her hair sticking up in a cowlick where her head was jammed against one of the pillows.

So why did I still have this awful feeling?

"Mom?" I said.

She mumbled.

I went in and flopped down on the bed next to her. "Hey," I said. "Are you still sleeping?"

She rolled over and blinked at me. My mom has spectacular eyes, the only really *green* eyes I've ever seen. "Umm," she said vaguely.

"Listen, Mom. Did Gran call this morning?"

" 'Course not," she said. "Lost, your Gran. Prob'ly can't remember our phone number."

Her eyes were tearing up. I changed the subject. "How was your date last night?"

Mom sighed and rolled away from me a little, staring up at the ceiling. "Mmm," she said.

"Did you like the skating?"

"Skating." She sighed. "Beautiful."

She stretched, yawned, sat up in her nightgown, and reached for her robe, moving in a strange sort of lazy motion. She got up and wandered over to the full-length mirror on her closet door.

The cowlick stood up right over her ear. Normally she would have sworn at it and tried to brush it down right away. Today she just stood there, swaying a little, and gawping at the mirror.

She had her shadow, I could see that. What she didn't have was her reflection.

Or rather, the reflection that I saw—though I bet nobody but Gran or me would have seen it—was of my mom in her jeans and ski jacket, on ice skates, turning in a slow, blind circle with closed eyes.

"Mom!" I screamed. I pulled her away from the mirror.

"What's the matter?" she said in a blurred, irritable voice, pushing my hands away. She turned back toward the mirror. She sat down on the end of her bed and just stared at her crazy, fake reflection.

"Mom," I said.

"Sshh," she said, not even looking at me. " 'M busy."

I retreated to the kitchen, where I sat hunched up in a chair trying to keep from exploding in tears. Gran had given me this one thing to do, and I'd failed, failed, failed. So instead of my mom, my real mom, I had this—this weird, drippy, zombie-mom who came padding barefoot into the kitchen after me and stood looking aimlessly around.

"Sit down," I said angrily. She was blinking at the window—at her godawful reflection in the windowpane, of course! I kept my back turned to the glass. "I'll make you some coffee and stuff," I said.

"Oh, no," she said, "no coffee. Spiced tea, maybe. 'N some chicken curry."

"What?" I said. "You hate Indian food!"

She frowned and shook her head.

"I'm going out," I said desperately. "I'm going to see Lennie." No reaction. "Lennie," I said more loudly. "Remember Lennie, with one solid eyebrow? We're meeting at the Port Authority Bus Terminal and we're running away together!"

"Don't forget your . . ." Mom began, then forgot what I wasn't supposed to forget and stood there swaying slightly with her mouth open.

"My *what*?" I bawled. "Don't forget my *what*?"

"Your grandmother," she murmured, looking at me with unfocused eyes. "Your grandmother wouldn't understand."

"It's me that doesn't understand," I said, still hoping for some kind of breakthrough. It was like trying to reach somebody through yards of thick, murky water.

She smiled. "Wait till you're older, darling," she said, and she padded over to the window to see herself better (her enchanted self, her lost self). She began to hum a tune, if you could call it that—a kind of whiny drone in three-quarter time, through her nose.

The weird thing was, there were times I'd have been delighted for my mom to just sort of not notice me, not keep track of where I was or who I was with or how long I was on the phone or whatever. Only not now, and not like this. Actually having a mother who literally didn't know I was there, or care when this notion did penetrate her bemused consciousness for a second or two, was not the blast it was in daydreams. Nothing like it.

Worst of all, Gran hadn't called. And Mom was—well, like this.

Stick by your mother, Gran had said, in that case. Well, I couldn't. I couldn't stand it. I ran out of the apartment, slamming the door behind me.

What was I going to do? Call the cops and tell them that my mother was missing? She wasn't, not unless you *knew*. You can bet that Brightner had put a glamour on her too so that nobody else would notice her weird reflection. What in the world would they make of it if they did anyway? Not the truth, that was for sure.

I stuffed my hands in my pockets and walked hard and fast with my head down, going no place. He had her, all right. What was left was hardly even my mom anymore, and I just couldn't stand it.

You have to understand, my mom was this person who, if you jumped in her bed on a Sunday morning, would ask you to scratch her back, or she'd tell you her dreams and ask about yours. Or she would send you to bring in the Sunday paper from the mat outside the apartment door, so the two of you could spread it out all over the floor and do the crossword puzzle together over breakfast.

Maybe if I went back with the paper? Not a chance. Even the *New York Times* had no strength against Brightner's magic.

And without Gran, neither did I.

I walked over to the park, which was full of Sunday strollers and bicyclers and skateboarders and so on. The day had turned warmer, though the wind still blew. I walked down to the Wollman Ice Skating Rink.

What I saw when I got there was a little muddy-floored valley cupping at its sunken center a long, low building along the edge of a flat, bleached platter of concrete. The site was enclosed in a chain-link fence with a big gap torn in it, naturally, by the vandals the fence was supposed to keep out; and it was totally deserted. People seemed to avoid that part of the park, maybe because the broken-down skating rink was depressing to look at.

I wriggled through the gap in the fence and walked along the front of the building, looking down the barren face of the slab. The building itself was divided into large rooms with big windows and locked doors. It looked as if no one had done any work there for days, though the fat herringbone tracks in the soft earth around the slab seemed to indicate that maybe the Parks Department or somebody parked heavy machinery there, inside the torn fence.

No way could I conjure the image, let alone the reality, of my poor mom skating here with Dr. Brightner. I turned away and walked out of the park.

My mom, my real mom, was lost and I wanted her *back*. I stomped down Broadway, jostling people without even noticing, repeating over and over to myself, "I want her back, I want her back."

There was only one possibility. I had to reach Gran, somehow, to tell her that Brightner had moved with a speed and boldness that she just had not foreseen. He hadn't been able to "nobble" my Gran, so he'd nobbled Mom instead.

I should go back home and wait in case Gran called after all. What if she already had called, and only the poor ruin of my mom was there to answer? But I could not go back and see Mom like that. Anyway, I was so hungry, I couldn't even think. If I didn't eat something soon I was going to pass out.

I trudged over to Fifth Avenue, where street vendors with food carts cluster on the corners to handle business people on the run on weekdays and shoppers on weekends. In particular there are these delicious little shrimp dumplings, four for a dollar, with hot vinegar, which a person could gladly die for.

As I walked hopelessly along, sniffing the air for the aroma of dumplings, suddenly the buildings on my right opened out and I heard music.

I turned my head and looked down the line of trees in marble planters that leads to the heart of Rockefeller Plaza, where the sunken skating rink is.

Skating rink.

With no clear idea in my mind, I headed down the plaza toward the huge golden statue of Prometheus floating in golden ribbons of cloud. He's stuck up on the wall behind the rink, gazing down benevolently on the ice. He looks young, smooth, pleased with himself, and dumb.

I came to the rail on the near side of the rink, leaned over between two of the flagpoles that march all along the walls, and looked down.

There was no ice. The rink was still in its summer form, which is an outdoor café. I sagged against the railing, listening to some tourists laughing and talking as they took pictures of each other with golden Prometheus in the background.

Something weird and terrible began to happen.

The music on the loudspeaker system began to fade away, as if somebody had wrapped the speakers in layers of cotton. At the same time, the bright green and white stripes of the café umbrellas dimmed in front of my eyes. All the color seemed to be sucked out of what I saw—the flags snapping on the tall poles above the rink, the coats and jackets of people along the wall looking down, even golden Prometheus himself—like a photograph being developed very quickly, getting darker and darker.

Hunger, I thought. You've waited too long to eat, you're about to faint.

Then everything started to spin very slowly. Imagine looking into a very old, very slow clothes dryer, and all the clothes are black or gray.

I clutched the rail.

The center of what I was seeing started to brighten again while the rest got darker. I tried to hang on to the bright center. As I struggled to stay conscious to *see* it, I realized that what I was looking at was ice.

A shining disc of white ice, with night all around it and a dark crowd of people skating on it in absolute silence. No music, no laughing or shouting, no sound of skates scraping and hissing on the ice. No color—a silent black-and-white movie. People in dark clothes with shadowed faces swept soundlessly by without looking up or at each other or at anything.

I watched them, paralyzed. Frigid air seemed to pour up off that sparkling ice to freeze me where I stood.

I had a very slow, cold thought: this isn't the Rockefeller

rink. The Rockefeller rink is small. This is huge, with too many skaters, and it's so dark all around the ice.

The shadowy figures pulled away gradually from the clear center of the ice, which was marked off by a circle of traffic cones. They were bright orange, splashes of almost painful color. In that space in the center where color still lived, I saw Dr. Brightner and my mother skating together, all by themselves.

Not my real mother that I'd left at the apartment but a sort of water-paint image of her, translucent and delicate: her reflection, yet solid enough for him to hold her by the hand. They made a slow, weaving sort of dance together, she in her blue jeans and ski jacket and the purple wool hat she had pulled down over her hair, and Brightner in the three-piece suit that he wore to school. He didn't look silly or out of place. He looked powerful.

I wanted to shout, "Mom, Mom, look up, look at me— here I am!"

But I didn't. I was afraid Brightner would hear me, and *he* would look up at me. I would be captured too and drawn down onto the ice where I would skate forever and ever around the two of them, helpless and silent and cold.

Besides, I had to keep trying to remember, that wasn't my real mother down there. It was her magic reflection, the very special fetch Brightner had made for her.

My mother has never really been a sporty person. All her athletic crazes lasted just as long as it took her to decide that the type of man who did that particular sport wasn't for her.

Now every move she made on the ice was perfect, like the moves of an Olympic athlete. Her eyes were closed. Her face, when she turned so that I could see it, had an expression of bliss. She looked young and beautiful.

This was the reflection I'd seen in my mother's mirror. But which was more real, more alive: the mindless mom-doll drifting around our apartment, or this dreaming image down below me?

If I cried, my tears would blur this vision. I clutched the rail with both hands and opened my eyes as wide as I could, even though I was scared that my eyeballs were freezing slowly in their sockets from staring and staring at the ice.

Brightner let go of Mom's hand and drifted back from her a little. She didn't even try to get away from him. He put his hands behind his back and skated in a circle around her while she made these slow, perfect loops at the very center of the ice. He turned and turned around her, his face always toward her, like a tiger circling a deer.

With no effort, he controlled it all: his own gliding steps, the others drifting dimly past his back, and my mother herself, who had never in her life looked like that, moved like that, smiled like that. Never.

Now he did look up, and he grinned at me, a big, wide, taunting grin.

Everything went gray and woolly and I started to topple over.

I hung onto the railing for dear life. Music broke over my head like a wave—and a siren, car horns, the metal catches on the flag ropes clinking against the flagpoles in the light breeze. And the laughter of two women down below at a café table under a green and white umbrella.

9

Against Orders

When I could get my legs to work again, I ran home. Mom was there, just as I had left her, mooning around in her nightgown like the heroine of one of the dippy romances that two of her authors wrote. She hadn't bothered to answer the phone all day. There were six messages on the answering machine, not one of them from Gran.

I could only think of one thing to do: the thing Gran had told me not to do, of course. I had to go find her at Collie's Kitchen. I slapped some peanut butter on a heel of rye bread and called information.

There was no such restaurant listed, according to the operator. A heavy cloud of despair settled over me. On the other hand—if you could have The Olde Salte Seller, why not cutesify the name of a restaurant? I said, "Maybe both words begin with a K?"

I heard the computer clicking and the operator said

doubtfully, "I do show a restaurant with a name like that, spelled with a K."

"Ha!" I said, hopeful again.

"It's not 'Collie,'" said the operator. "I show K-A-L-I, Kali's Kitchen. Could that be what you're looking for?"

It hit me: not "Collie" as in *Lassie Come Home,* but *Kali,* the terrible Indian goddess of death and destruction!

I remembered her from our English class unit on Mythologies of the World last year. Kali is a horrible aspect of a powerful goddess. She has four arms and huge tusks and wears necklaces of snakes, skulls, babies' heads, and so on, which gives you some idea of her disposition. Her tongue hangs out about a foot and drips blood. I had had a couple of rousing nightmares about her during that study unit.

"Are you there?" I shouted into the phone. "Operator, I don't want the number, I just need the address!"

I scribbled the information on a napkin, hung up, and took off like a rocket, heading across town and down on the East Side toward where the streets start to turn seedy.

And there it was, on a block with a bakery, closed; a liquor store, closed; a tiny little hole-in-the-wall grocery, open and very high-priced; a hat store for men, closed; a magazine store, open, with foreign magazines and several men clustered near the cash register where they kept the girlie magazines; and a tiny French café.

I walked that block about six times before I got up the nerve to approach the place I was looking for, with its big front window and faded red awning: *Kali's Kitchen,* it read, in curly white script.

I leaned close to read the speckled, sun-dried menu taped inside the window next to two ancient newspaper reviews. The sign on the door said, Open. I peeked in the window, over a table draped in a red cloth with a little vase of drooping flowers on it. Somewhere deep inside in the gloom, somebody moved around.

Brightner?

70

I beat a quick retreat across the street and stood behind a lamppost like a dummy (even I am not *that* thin).

A little Indian lady in a pink sari looked out of the restaurant doorway, up and down the street. She had a thick braid of black hair and a flash of gold at her ear. Did she see me?

She held the door for a couple of patrons and went inside with them, and I started breathing again.

Now what? If Gran was still around here someplace, spying on Brightner (and she had to be, she was my only hope), she'd be in some kind of disguise. So how was *I* going to spot her?

I waited for hours, loafing in the magazine store and hoping every time somebody went in or out of Kali's Kitchen that it would turn out to be Gran and wouldn't turn out to be Brightner.

At dinnertime a steady stream of street people made their way into the alley that ran alongside the restaurant building. They were let in through a side door that was propped ajar. That was how Dirty Rose and Gran must have gone in for their meal last night.

Gran must still be in there. Maybe she was pretending to be a new waitress, or a kitchen hand. Maybe she was busy going through secret files in some back-room office with a little camera, like a movie spy. *Granny Gran and the Restaurant of Doom.*

My job: find her! But how? I came up with the bright idea of making my first effort as a burglar.

Having no handy disguises with me and not knowing whether Brightner himself was inside, I could hardly march in the front door. I would have to sneak in through the side entrance, sometime before the place was locked up for the night.

I stayed across the street in the shadow of the magazine-store doorway with my hands in my jacket pockets, hopping from one foot to another to keep warm. My running shoes were not so great for standing around in cold weather. I only

71

left once, to dash up the block and buy a couple of sticks of shish kebab from a street vendor for my dinner. Then I waited some more.

This was not at all like coming out of a late movie with Barb, say; or wandering around with some kids from school down in the Village. This wasn't like anything I knew.

To tell the truth, I was not used to being out, on my own or in company, so late. The yellow pools of the street lights with all that dark in between, the sounds of traffic whizzing brightly past on the avenue up at the end of the street, and the closed and silent storefronts left and right and across from me all seemed very sinister.

Also my ears were *freezing*. By this time it was very chilly and very dark, and there was barely any traffic, foot or wheeled, on the street.

Suddenly I heard voices calling in a foreign language, and a door slammed in the alley. A skinny little guy in a leather jacket came out of the dark and walked quickly away down the street. A few minutes later two black-haired women left, chatting and laughing, also by the side door.

I looked at my watch: it was one-thirty in the morning.

Quiet again, except for a car horn far off somewhere and a faint sound of barking. I tried to think, but my brain felt like ice floating between my icicle ears.

Two more people came out of Kali's Kitchen with bikes and rode away on them. I heard someone sing out after them, "Good night, good night, don't be late tomorrow," from inside the alley doorway.

How many staff people could they crowd into that little restaurant?

I couldn't stand it anymore. It was now or never.

Now.

I ran across the street and into the alley. The side door opened easily and quietly. I dashed inside, past a glimpse of the bright, empty kitchen with swinging doors in the far wall leading out to the dining area, where somebody might still be cleaning up.

I flung myself down the stairs into the basement. They were steel steps, with little leaf-design treads embossed on them to keep your feet from slipping. A bicycle leaned into the corner of the landing halfway down.

In the basement, a double door stood partially open. I looked back up the stairs. I'd done it, committed myself: now what if Pink Sari or Brightner himself sneaked up behind me and trapped me down here?

Don't think about it.

I flattened myself against one of the metal doors and peeked inside.

No Claw, no Brightner, no Sari, even, but an odor strong enough to knock out a water buffalo: a mixture of heavy spices, sweaty clothing, and stale liquor. I held my breath and looked into a large room lit only by the dim light spilling in from behind me: bare walls, a cement floor with cracks in it, and high along the walls a few small, grimy, barred windows.

The floor was covered with what I thought were rows of rag bundles. Against the far wall someone had set up a table supporting two big steel pots. The only other item of "furniture" was a large, overflowing garbage can in one corner with a litter of Styrofoam bowls scattered around its base.

One of the bundles coughed and rolled and flung out an arm. Another one groaned and swore. Now that I listened, I could hear them breathing: sleeping people, homeless people who had come in here at dinnertime for a meal and a place to spend the night out of the cold. Looking carefully, I could see holey shoe-soles sticking out of one end of the nearest bundle.

There was another sound, an odd sound, from above my head. It was a sort of rolling, thumping noise, like small boats tied at a dock when a big swell or a wind comes along and bumps them against the pilings. Nothing especially scary in that, so why was the skin at the back of my neck crawling? Because boats don't float in basements.

So what did? I squinted up at the ceiling. It was hidden in darkness.

Then a flicker of movement attracted my attention. At first I thought somebody was getting up to go look for the bathroom.

A shadowy form rose from where one sleeper lay, but as I watched I saw that the lumpish, sleeping shape didn't change. The rising form was just a dim figure like a cutout, drawing itself out of the sleeper and drifting upward toward the ceiling. There it hung, turning and rolling and bumping slowly with a horrible nightmare motion among another dozen shadows like itself, which I had taken for a single layer of ordinary nighttime gloom.

Before my eyes two more shadows drifted upward. I could see the window through one of them.

Understanding bloomed silently inside me like a poison flower: in the morning, the bleary-eyed bums would be wakened and sent away. They would shamble off wondering why they felt a little weird, maybe thinking that Indian food didn't agree with them. Sometime later Brightner would come down into the supposedly empty basement room. He would reach up (with what? a broom? a magic Claw?) and hook the helpless, bobbing shadows down one by one, and send them to join the crowd in the phantom rink.

One shadow, livelier than the others, scrabbled wildly but soundlessly at the ceiling with its fingers. I thought I could make out the lumpy profile of Dirty Rose.

I turned and fled up the stairs, thinking only of getting *out*.

The door to the alley had been closed and locked.

I was shut in with the lady with the sari, and the sleepers in the basement and the phantoms that were oozing out of them.

Not having a lot of other options, I got a grip on myself, more or less. I tried to take stock. Here at street level, I could look straight into the kitchen. There was not a soul in sight.

I listened hard. I heard tap water dripping, and faint

74

twangy piped music, and somebody walking around on the floor above my head—soft steps, quick and light. Pink Sari, probably. Should I be afraid of her? If she was mixed up with Brightner, yes.

The footsteps stopped and I heard someone sigh and the creaking of a chair. Pink Sari or someone was busy doing the day's accounts or whatever you do after a restaurant has closed its doors for the night.

What now? In the stairwell below, the handlebars of the last lone bike gleamed. The idea of the lady in the sari riding her wheels home in the middle of the night should have made me smile. It didn't. My mouth, my whole self was cramped with fear.

I opened a very unimportant-looking door on my right. Strong smells, exotic and overwhelming, washed over me. I looked into a narrow pantry of shelves loaded with plastic buckets labeled in black Magic Marker: "Gum," "cloves," "mango powder," "ground cumin seed," "black cumin," "black mustard," "green cardamom," "black cardamom," "black salt."

"Black" flavorings? Black magic! Hastily, I shut the door.

I crossed the spotless, gleaming kitchen and went out through the swinging doors into a short passageway that had a sign, *Restrooms,* and two doors, right and left. Nobody was in either of the restrooms.

The dining area of the restaurant was two large dim rooms full of round tables with chairs upended on them. An illuminated exit sign gleamed red over a fire door on my left. A partition topped with a row of potted plants marked off the two dining rooms from each other.

I padded quietly around, taking a look under the tables, behind the bar, inside the tiny hatcheck room. Beside the cash register was a dish of the same little seed-candies Brightner kept on his desk at school. I could smell them: sugary licorice, sweet and inviting, but the one thing every kid who's ever read a fairy tale knows is, when you're in the ogre's castle, don't eat anything, or you'll be stuck there forever.

I turned away from the candies and saw the painting on the wall behind me. I had to jam my knuckles in my mouth to stifle a screech.

Above the booths along the back wall someone had painted a life-sized monster with tusks, a bloody tongue, a yellow necklace of cut-off heads with closed eyes, and four flexed arms: Kali, dancing with curled toes on a heap of people she was trampling underfoot.

How in the world could I see her so clearly in this dim, after-hours light? But I did. She capered, brandishing her clawlike hands, glowing somehow with her own light, and leering into the dining room with eyes like two billiard balls.

How could anybody sit under that thing and eat a meal? Of course, if you sat under it you wouldn't actually *see* it without craning your neck.

I made myself walk over and touch the paint on the wall. That's all it was: paint on a wall.

Hot paint, hot to the touch!

As I snatched my hand away, something moved up there: a quick flicker of motion in the middle of Kali's forehead. In one blink, an eye appeared, a wide, rolling, bloodshot eye right above the meeting point of the painted eyebrows—the third eye of Kali, staring right at me!

The piped music blared out an ear-splitting shriek with wobbles in it, like maniacal laughter.

In a panic I bolted for the alley door, crashing into tables and sending chairs flying on my way. The door was just as locked as it had been before.

Light steps came pattering down the stairs. Where to go—the basement, with the shadows bobbing against the ceiling? Not on your life.

I yanked open the door to the spice room and leaped in. The door shut behind me, closing me in with utter blackness and warm, odorous air.

Outside, two quick steps—and a key turned in the lock.

Trapped! Whimpering, I flapped around in that narrow,

stuffy space, gasping for breath as if I were suffocating, and knocking the plastic tubs every which way.

Someone who I guessed to be Pink Sari called to me from the other side of the door in this light, musical voice: "Are you all right, young lady? You will be Valentine, isn't it? I was told that you might come. Are you all right? My husband would be very upset with me if he found you hurt in any way."

Her husband?

"Who?" I squeaked.

"But you have met him," she said, all tinkling and social, "at your school."

I had fallen into the hands of the Bride of Brightner.

10

Specialty of the House

"You'd better let me out," I croaked. "I'm feeling terrible. I've got a bad heart."

"Oh, don't say such a thing of yourself!" she cried sweetly. "I am sure you are of very good heart indeed."

"My boyfriend is outside, waiting for me," I threatened in a squeaky voice; and I couldn't help thinking of Lennie, who was pretty big and strong for his age, but not, unfortunately, either my boyfriend or outside.

A delighted chuckle from beyond the door: "Oh, I am trembling—but only a little. If this fine boyfriend so fears to face me that he lets you come here alone, will he be brave enough to face my husband?"

I unpeeled my fingers from the wooden upright of the spice shelves and felt my way to the door, where I sat down because my legs wouldn't hold me. I was now in an icy sweat of pure terror.

"Where is he?" I said. "Your—your husband?"

"I do not ask my husband where he goes or when he comes back," she said. "It is for him to tell me what he thinks I should know."

Trying to flatten out the tremor in my voice, I said firmly, "Well, maybe he doesn't think you should know this, but I think you should. He's dating my mother!"

There was a moment's silence. Then she sighed, a fetching little sound of womanly knowingness and resignation. It made me want to gag.

"But this is only a seeming thing," she said. "I am the true wife, the one he keeps by him always and comes back to always. A little 'dating' is completely nothing."

Maybe she actually didn't *know* what kind of monster she was married to?

"If he's such a nice guy, then what's he got going downstairs," I said, "people sleeping while those—those . . . ?" I didn't know what to call the shadows.

"Oh, those?" she said casually. "Mere shavings off the soul, totally harmless, of course."

"I'll bet," I said, with a shudder I couldn't control. I was glad she couldn't see me. "How do you—make them come out of the people?"

"The food makes a special sleep. While our guests sleep, they dream. They dream their fears, and flying from them, they fly out of their bodies a little. The part that flies out, the fear, is gathered by my husband so that the lucky sleeper wakes refreshed and relieved of all this fearfulness. He brings great peace to so many troubled souls this way."

In a pig's eye, I thought. Could she really be so innocent? I wanted to think so. That would mean that at least I had some chance of persuading her to let me go before Brightner came back from Buffalo or ice-skating or wherever he was.

"He's sure got a nice deal worked out," I said. "He chases other women while you stay here and run things for him."

She laughed. "Of course, this is the way things are.

Men, even great men, even such men who have found their destined mate and partner, even they have this urge to pursue other ladies. It has happened before, but it is Ushah he comes back to, it is Ushah who stays with him. All the others he puts away, one after the other."

"All?" I said, horrified all over again. "How many are there?"

"Oh, I don't even bother to keep count," she said airily. "It doesn't matter, you see."

Like heck it didn't! I was talking with the number-one wife of Bluebeard. And he was after my mom. After, nothing—he had her!

The rich spice smell was making me a little sick to my stomach; or maybe it was just fear. I shouted, "Well, whatever he *usually* does with his—his ladies and those other poor people, he won't get away with it this time!"

"Oh, my poor husband," she mocked. "To have you so angry with him! He will explain to you when he comes, and then you can apologize for these rude things you are saying. Luckily for you, he will be in a very good mood when I tell him how you came by all on your own, after hours, when there was no one around to notice if you got yourself locked in the spice pantry."

I heard her walking away. I yelled after her, but she didn't come back.

Well, there was some comfort: she might have poor Dirty Rose down there in the basement, but she didn't have Gran. She'd have boasted of it if she did.

On the other hand, she did have me. I had to find a way out of the spice pantry.

I started by checking over every inch of it in the pitch-darkness. There weren't a whole lot of inches. I even pulled down some of the spice buckets and climbed up the shelves to try getting the one tiny window open. The window was completely painted over and jammed shut. It wouldn't budge. I tried for a long time.

Eventually I conked out. I remember feeling hopelessly

80

convinced that I would never see the light of day again, except past the bulk of my deadly enemy, Dr. Brightner.

I woke up very thirsty and with a runny nose and eyes that itched like crazy. I was allergic to something in here. Sitting by the locked door, I sniffled like a baby, shaking and scared. I couldn't even tell what time it was. My watch has little luminous points on it for the hours, but they need some kind of light bouncing off them to show up. In that hole of a room—well, if not for the absolutely overwhelming smell of those spices, you could have used the place for a sensory deprivation experiment.

I wasn't going to be found looking all wet and runny like a little kid by piggy old Brightner if I could help it. I began hunting through my pockets for something to blow my nose on.

I found something. I found the silver glove.

As soon as my fingers closed on that soft, crumply leather, I had to smother an angry shout of laughter: what a jerk I was! What a relief that Gran wasn't here with me to *see* what a jerk I was!

The first thing I should have insisted that she teach me about the glove was to remember, in a pinch, that I had it! Which is not something that comes naturally to a person raised in a world that doesn't believe in magic. For example, when tough kids start following you in the park in New York, the first thing you think is not likely to be, gosh, have I got my magic glove with me?

You panic. I had panicked. It was now time to get unpanicked and try seriously using my head.

I put on the silver glove and I whispered to it, "I need to get out of here! Help!"

The glove seemed to hug my hand like a promise.

I pressed my ear against the door and listened. Something had wakened me, and pretty soon I heard it again: running steps, shrill curses in an accented voice, and great thumpings on the walls. What was Ushah up to? And did I really want to know? I imagined her beating the dust out of the poor lost shadows.

"—Dirty creature!" she shouted as she passed the door in a rushing swish of silk. Then came another screeched curse. Whatever it was about, the fuss seemed to have taken her out of the immediate vicinity.

Not daring to breathe, I turned the doorknob slowly with my gloved hand. The latch slipped softly free without even a click. In a burst of confidence, I opened the door and stepped out of the spice pantry into what seemed by comparison to be wonderfully cool, fresh air.

The kitchen was empty, lit only by daylight from one window. Afternoon light—I checked my watch. I had slept for something like fourteen hours! A black sleep from those black-magical spices, so here it was Monday afternoon.

On Mondays lots of restaurants in New York are closed. Ushah was probably alone here, and for the moment not nearby. I could hear the sounds of muffled pursuit down in the basement.

Good—whatever was running from Ushah, it would help keep her busy down there while I checked the office upstairs for signs of Gran. Which I meant to do immediately, before I could think about it and chicken out.

First, though, I had to be sure there was a way out of this place. Shutting the spice pantry door behind me, I headed for the side door, which was still shut and locked. The silver glove would take care of that, I was sure. The doorknob turned slowly, but it did turn.

Increasing noise from below: I ducked behind some crates stacked in the passageway, my heart hammering. Ushah was making such a racket herself that it would take more than a thundering heartbeat to get her attention. I hoped.

A small animal streaked wildly up the stairs. Then came Ushah, wielding a mop and yelling. She cornered the creature—it was a gray cat, all puffed up and spitting with fear and rage—at the door to the pantry.

With her back to me Ushah moved in on the cat,

snarling softly, "When I find which one let you in—oh, such stupid people! Feeding you on the sly, hey? Telling each other how you will keep mice away. 'Health inspector' means nothing to them, I have to think of everything! Well, you won't steal food here again!"

The cat ducked an Olympic-powered whack of the mop and tore back down into the basement with Ushah pursuing in full cry.

I gathered my nerve for a quick run upstairs to the office—and a prickling sensation rolled through my sinuses. I grabbed my nose and pinched it hard—too late! I was blown backward by an enormous sneeze.

In the one second of silence that ensued, I clambered to my feet and made a break for the alley door in a crash of toppling crates. Flinging open the door, I tore out into the light of a clear, late New York afternoon.

I couldn't do anything for Gran here now. Or for myself, either. I am a fast runner. I ran.

"Stop, *thief*!" shrieked Ushah, the Bride of Brightner. That voice would have turned a charging bull, and for a second it turned me, or my head anyway, while my feet kept flying.

Out of the doorway behind me, soaring over the tumbled crates, came a fury in pink. She sat sidesaddle on a bicycle that spun madly down the alley after me, glittering with a light of more than polished chrome.

I knew The Claw when I saw it.

Never have I run like that. Never, ever, have I dodged and slid and zipped so madly and dangerously through the narrowest gaps between people and cars, and trucks parked two-deep in the narrow crosstown streets.

The bike darted behind me, leaping obstructions like a skeleton horse, skidding on its tires as it sped on my trail carrying Ushah in her gossamer pink sari. Like some colorful Indian fantasy of a western witch on her broomstick, she flew after me on a bike that she didn't need to pedal with her dainty feet. Her face was the snarling face of Kali.

83

Now I knew who had flown the killer kite in Central Park when Gran and I rode the flying carpet! Ushah sat the jumps like an equestrienne champ and screamed like a banshee, "Thief! Thief! Stop, thief!"

God, the unfairness of it—she, who helped her husband steal people's souls, calling *me* a thief!

For once there was some justice in this world. New Yorkers are cautious about getting mixed up in other people's business. People turned to stare but nobody tried to stop me. I zigzagged like a streak of lightning, heading for the only sanctuary I could think of.

Like a lot of shops in New York, The Makeup Stop has a locked street door. You ring and wait to be let in.

Not me. I whacked the door handle with the silver glove, flung myself inside, and slammed the door behind me. I stood panting in the pretty little mirror-walled boutique which belonged to the mother of my friend Barb. With Ushah's screech building up outside as she came zooming after me, I dove past the counter and between the print curtains into the back room.

Barbara jumped up from a little desk wedged into a corner where she had her looseleaf notes open next to her math text. She is the only person I know who actually starts her homework when she gets in from school instead of waiting as long as possible.

"What?" she said.

I could only point behind me and shake my head frantically, having no breath to utter a single word.

Barb yanked open the warped plywood door to the tiny bathroom just as the bell over the front door gave, if you can imagine it, a furious tinkle. I fell into the minuscule bathroom and slumped down on the toilet lid, trying to get some air into my lungs and not die of the cramp in my side.

I was safe for the moment, assuming Ushah couldn't just smash her way in and demolish the flimsy bathroom door to get at me.

Barb was somebody I used to play horsey with, running

around on the roof of her little brownstone apartment building with one of us holding a length of clothesline in her
mouth for bit and reins. When it came time for the other one
to be the horse and do her paces and chase outlaws and all
that, well, whichever one of us it was would chomp down on
the same damp place in the rope without flinching. We were
that close.

I shook with relief. I may actually have passed out for a
minute there. The next thing I knew, Barb was yelling in my
ear.

"Hey," she said, "hey, Valentine, who is that crazy lady?
What's going on? You look wrecked, girl!"

"Is she gone?" I gasped.

"She's backed off for now," Barb said. "Come on out of
here. This place was not designed for two."

I tiptoed fearfully out of the tiny bathroom into the back
room, peeking past the curtain into the shop. "Where is she?
She didn't just *leave*!"

"She's hanging around across the street," Barb said.
"Look from here, can you see her?"

"I don't want to see her," I moaned.

Barb gave me a critical look. "You better tell me what's
happening, quick, before my mom comes back."

"Got anything to eat?" I said, looking longingly at the
little half-fridge next to the desk. "I'm dying of thirst, too."

She handed me a diet soda and a wilted ham sandwich,
which I gobbled.

"Okay," she said. "Why is that lady hot on your trail,
anyway? One thing I've learned the hard way, it's just like
they say: what goes around, comes around. So why is this
person coming around after you?"

"Honestly, Barb, it's not my fault! I didn't do anything
to anybody!"

"Okay," she said. "So who did what to you, then?"

Not really knowing how or where to begin, I blurted,
"It's Brightner. It's all Brightner's fault! He's a creep, a creepy,
lousy, dangerous creep!"

"Yeah?" said Barb. "He make a move on you, or what?"

I was about to say, a move on my mother, and me, and in a way even my Gran, but it sounded so *gross*. Also a certain amount of caution held me back. It was a lot of years since Barb and I had played horsey.

So I temporized. "It's a secret, Barb," I said. "A super-saturated-seven-times-secret."

This was a formula we'd used as kids for our spy games. Barb grinned and said, "Double-defended and never revealed." Our countersign!

Well, after that, I had to tell her the whole thing. I mean *all* of it.

Barb said, "Huh," and, "Uh," and other things like that, which ran a gamut of expression from total disbelief to thoughtful consideration by the time I got through.

She looked me up and down and shook her head. "You don't look any crazier than usual, but that is some story: Valentine and the Demon Shrink! Tell you one thing, that lady was all set to bite my face off."

"What did you say to her?" I said. Barb is so tall and so smooth- and self-possessed-looking that she can pull off a lot of things I wouldn't dream of even trying.

She said, "Well, she came running up after you and set to screaming at me through the door, which did not make a good impression. I screamed back that we're closed, which we will be, at least until Mom gets back."

"She was running?" I said. "On her own two feet?"

"Well, what else, cloven hooves?" Barb said.

"Barb," I said, "I wouldn't be surprised."

11

Dressed
for Success

I closed my eyes and tried to think. Where was The Claw? I couldn't stay here forever, certainly not until Barb's mom came. She wouldn't know that she shouldn't let Ushah in, that she wasn't just another customer. But how could I leave without being caught? "Where is your mom?" I said.

Barb cut her eyes at me. "Taking care of things." Which probably meant Mrs. Wilson was off arguing with some authority or other about something Barb's brother got caught doing, which happened a lot. If you wanted to stay friends with Barb, you learned not to ask.

"If she comes back and lets Ushah in, I'm a dead duck," I said.

Barb said, "Why not just sock Ushah with this magic glove of yours?"

I could tell that Barb was dying to see the glove in action. Her idea had a certain amount of instant appeal, but only in the abstract. To tell the truth, I could not face the idea of getting within reach of Ushah again, glove or no glove.

Luckily I had a perfectly rational objection. "Barb, I have no idea what might happen—maybe a nuclear meltdown! I just don't know enough to risk it. I mean, how would your mom like to come back here and find nothing but a scorched crater where the shop used to be?"

Barb gave up. "If you're all that worried, there is a back door, remember? Opens into that hall by the hotel coffee shop."

Ahah! Maybe. I said, "Take a look out there first. Don't let—don't let anything in, okay? But tell me what you find."

She stepped around the rack of clothes her mother kept in back for models to use. I heard the door to the hall open and then shut again, quietly. Barb came back looking thoughtful.

"There's a bike out there," she said. "Now, who would take the risk of leaving a bike like that alone in New York with no chain or anything?"

And we both said together, "Who but the Bride of Brightner?"

Barb went back to the possible powers of the silver glove, which had not made me invisible to Ushah when that was what I most dearly needed, nor turned into a magic carpet and flown me away. I found this failure disappointing when I thought about it. Barb found it provocative.

She wanted to try the glove on, of course, to see if it would do anything special for her. I think she still suspected that I was crazy, but as a devoted science fiction and fantasy reader she hoped for the best.

I wouldn't let her try on the glove. Suppose it was tied to me alone by my Gran's gift? Suppose the glove did funny things to my friend that I couldn't fix afterward? I needed Barb in her present form with all her wits about her, not Barb transformed into a light bulb or a bat.

It was bad enough that I'd brought the awful Ushah to

her door. Barb didn't take that part nearly seriously enough—it wasn't her that Ushah had come roaring after like a Fury.

Barb sulked a little and muttered to herself about dumb messes that I wouldn't even help her help me out of. Then she got this cunning look and she said, "This claw thing: how does it follow you? I mean, it's by sight, right? It doesn't trail you like a hound, I mean."

"Sniff?" I said. "How? A bicycle has no nose."

"Well, it's got no eyes either, but it must have seen you to chase you like that."

"Unless Ushah was doing the seeing and she steers it somehow," I said, shuddering. I could still hear Ushah's outrageous shrieks of "Stop, thief!" in my head.

"Well, I bet even Ushah the Terrible doesn't have X-ray eyes," Barb said triumphantly. "And there's two ways out of here. Now, I'm not letting anybody in or out the front door till my mother gets here. But suppose somebody The Claw had never seen walked out the back way—out through the hotel lobby, where tons of people rush around all the time? Somebody Ushah the Ugly never saw before, either?"

I stared at her. I started to grin.

"An illusion," I said. "You mean fake him out—him *and* Ushah the Awful—with an illusion!"

Which meant, turn the tables on Brightner—play a trick on the magician, hoodwink the hoodwinker who had my mom hypnotized by an image of herself in the mirror! Deceive his horrible servants by pretending to be somebody else the way he deceived everybody by pretending to be my school psychologist—what was that but poetic justice?

Any kind of justice would do—I was dying for some—but could we pull it off? Could we fool Brightner's accomplice and Brightner's Claw in its bicycle form? Brightner was a rogue wizard who could go after you with coat hangers and kites, who could make ordinary things rise up against you in his service, until you were jellified with fear. Barb and I were just—well, us.

I whined a little about this, but Barb didn't see it that

way. She gave me this offended look. "Who said anything about illusion? When I get done with you, girl, you going to *be* somebody else!"

So there I sat getting myself made up by my best friend so that I could walk out right past my enemy without being recognized. And did Barb do a job on me!

I am tall and skinny and pale with what they call ash-blond hair; not bad, I guess, though I can always think of lots of improvements when I look in a mirror.

Barb is taller and thinner than I am. Her skin is about the shade of my aunt's teakwood dining table. Clothes of any cut or color look absolutely fabulous on Barb. In general she is gorgeous.

I once suggested that she should be a model, and she laughed. She told me that *a*, most successful black models have narrow, Arab-type faces, not her own broad-nosed looks and *b*, because her mother ran the makeup business Barb knew the models who shopped there, and from what she could gather, even when you *are* successful, it's a pretty pitsy life and no thanks. What she wants to be is a veterinarian, with a sideline in animal art.

On the other hand, what Barb doesn't know about cosmetics hasn't been dreamed up yet. When we were little kids we used to play in the back of her mother's boutique by the hour, trying on the clothes and the accessories and the shoes and so on, and slathering all kinds of gunk on our faces.

Now we did it in earnest, trying to get me transformed before Barb's mom showed up and let Ushah in.

First I had to take off my shirt, which frankly I was glad to get rid of. It was very grubby and permanently loaded with the smell of the spice room. You wouldn't *need* a nose to track it.

Same with my jeans. I sat at the back-room makeup table in a borrowed slip while Barb cleaned me up with cold cream, right down to my shoulders and my collarbone.

Well, she used everything—tissues and pads and pat-pat-pat, layers of liquid stuff brushed on and blotted dry, eyeliner and lip-liner and eyelashes glued onto my lids and new dimensions in eyebrows thanks to the eyebrow pencil. Her hands flew. I watched in the mirror and saw myself being turned into somebody else.

Barb sang and talked to herself, "Thundercats, ho!" and other tripe from the TV cartoons she watches (for the art, she says). She darkened my skin about six shades and made my eyes huge and my cheekbones immense and my mouth luscious and my nose narrow and arched and aristocratic (at least to look at, thanks to the shadows she brushed in on the sides). I became—who?

"How old you want to be?" she said, looking at my reflection with me.

"Twenty," I said.

"Thirty," Barb said firmly. So I got some bruisy-looking shadows under my eyes, little lines starting at the corners of my mouth, seams in my forehead and shadows on my neck.

"I don't believe this," I said. "I look just like my aunt Grace!"

Barb laughed. "You *did* look like Aunt Grace. Watch now. Hair," she said, "transform!"

Up went my long blond hair under a wig of black curls. I looked like a high-gloss poodle.

We did things with fake tanning stuff on my legs, to match my darkened face. Not my hands, though. I wouldn't take off the silver glove. Barb said, "Fine, be pigheaded. We'll take care of it later. Now, a blouse and skirt for you; the serious look. You a lawyer or a doctor?"

"I am a fugitive," I said. "From a crazed Indian witch."

"No you're not," Barb said. "You're an investment counselor, that's what you are. Give you some class and some brains. Oh-oh, who's that—is that my mom?"

The person looming momentarily outside the plate-glass window at the shop-front was not her mom, in fact, but a disappointed customer, willowy and pouty-mouthed. Still, for a second there the "investment counselor" almost lost it. I certainly gave up any inclination to argue the details or career plans of my new identity, which was getting kind of interesting.

So in an hour and a half, there I was, bending in knots to be able to see myself in the full-length mirrors without letting Ushah have a glimpse. We'd left the curtain partly open to keep an eye on *her*, actually, and so that we could keep watch for Barb's mom.

I wore the most beautiful tailored gray skirt ever seen, panty hose, and a silky white blouse with full sleeves under a blue velvet vest, and a blue velvet jacket.

"You're tall," Barb said, "so she'll be looking for tall, or somebody trying to look short. So let's make you *really* tall."

She found me some dark blue pumps with three-inch heels. I had to practice for ten minutes to make sure I wouldn't fall over. The last thing I needed now was a twisted ankle.

A short gray glove was found to match, more or less, the long one on my left hand. The sleeves of the blue jacket hid the difference in cuff lengths. Gold-plated chains looped down from my neck. We added a dark blue shoulder bag, a light raincoat, and a silvery scarf. Barb stood back and judged me ready.

"Your own shadow wouldn't know you," she said with satisfaction (which was not the best way of putting it just then).

In fact, I was pretty knocked out by the person I had become on the outside: capable, proud, wildly attractive! Could I ever look like that, really? *Be* like that? I was fascinated by what felt like a weird glimpse of my future—one possible future, anyway.

If this worked and I *had* a future.

"Listen," Barb said, "you're on your way to have drinks with six economic advisors to the President, all right? You got lots on your mind and no time to waste, which is how you walk and talk."

"Who's talking?" I said. "Nobody's getting close enough for long enough to talk."

"Yeah, well, just don't let anybody get close enough to smell you, because you still stink of curry."

"God," I groaned. "This isn't going to work, I know it isn't!"

Barb sniffed. "That's right," she said, "spoil it all by being a scaredy-cat."

"I'm not a scaredy-cat," I said. "I'm just *scared*. I'll mess up, I'll make a mistake and give myself away."

Barb rolled her eyes to heaven. "After all this fine work I just did on you? Here," she said, suddenly serious as she dug something out of her bag and held it out to me. It was a little round hand-mirror in a smooth brass frame that her mother sold in the shop, the kind for checking your makeup discreetly. "You're looking at the first thing out of the first carton of goods that my mom got when she started this place. She put this little mirror aside for me, and she gave it to me years ago when she started teaching me about makeup so I could help her in the store. First time I ever saw myself looking all grown up, like you look now, it was in this mirror. That time my mom made me up like an Egyptian princess, she said. I'll never forget it. Made me feel like I *could*, you know? Whatever needed doing, I could do it, 'cause I wasn't just some dumb-ass kid with a flat nose and thick lips."

"Don't talk about my best friend like that," I said.

Barb said, "Take this with you. I'm telling you, take it, girl! If you get shaky, look in there and be what you see, hear me? You've got it in you, or I couldn't bring it out like this, no matter how good I was. Go on, take the mirror. For luck."

I took it. I needed all the luck I could get.

The front door opened and closed. We went still as stone. "Barbara! Are you back there?"

Barb's mom.

"Just a minute!" Barb hollered. She grabbed the paper bag the ham sandwich had come in and shoved it into my hand. Then she opened the back door and hustled me out. The door shut behind me.

I was in a short hallway that dead-ended here at the shop and opened into the carpeted lobby of the hotel and the entrance to the coffee shop. Between that lobby and me, though, something lurked. I knew it lurked, though to anyone else the word "lurk" would not occur.

Against the wall, its front wheel crooked to hold it upright, leaned Ushah's bicycle. This was my first close look at it in good light. The seat was covered with what looked like tiger-hide, which made perfect sense to me. Twists of what seemed suspiciously like long black human hair hung from the handlebars. Not exactly the mount of a Hell's Angel—worse.

I felt my face begin to steam slightly with quivering dread. If I waited another second, I would melt all of Barb's work off.

Could I really walk past that thing, I mean stride past it like the woman I was made up to be, as if it were nothing but—a bike?

I patted my wig and took a good grip on the paper bag (I guessed it was supposed to hold whatever I'd been in the shop to buy). I threw out my chest and swung into what I hoped would be a convincing stride over the tile floor, snapping along with a real power-walk, like gunshots.

Wobbling loudly by The Claw in my incredible heels, I held myself in a grip of iron so as not to turn and look. Would an investment counselor on her way to hobnob with economists from Washington even notice a miserable bicycle in a hotel hallway? She would not.

As I passed it I heard a faint, tingling sound: the sound of the thin metal spokes vibrating slightly as the front wheel turned, following my progress, probing, questing after me.

Then I stepped onto the blood-red hotel carpeting and swept through that lobby as fast as I could on those heels, pretending like mad that I was hurrying toward something instead of running feverishly away. And in fact I was half-flying on the high I had gotten from making it this far. I stiff-armed the revolving door and emerged into the open air.

From the top step of the hotel entrance I saw Ushah. She stood in front of The Makeup Stop, glaring around with furious frustration. I froze. She would look right at me, she would see—

The door of the shop opened and Barb's mom looked out, said something. Ushah smiled and answered.

I might have stood there forever, frozen, watching with my breath held, but the hotel doorman caught my eye. He must have seen something he took for a signal—a flash of desperation, I bet—because he solemnly opened the door of the taxi at the curb and held it for me.

Somehow or other, a few seconds later I was sitting in the backseat of that cab, heading down the street. I craned my neck and stared fearfully out through the back window, but I saw no signs of a pink-wrapped Indian witch racing after me on The Claw.

12

The Demon Shrink

When I limped into the apartment in those torturous high heels, I found Mom in her room. She had taken down a suitcase from her closet and put it on her bed, and she was busy stuffing things into it at random—pages of manuscript, a couple of blouses she had previously laid out for ironing, her bedside clock, a half-full glass of water.

Worse, she was wearing her carpet slippers—the carpet slippers I had given her for Christmas. When she'd unwrapped the slippers she'd turned red and protested plaintively that she wasn't old enough for *carpet slippers*, for crying out loud. Then she'd spent the rest of the day trying to apologize to me for having thoughtlessly rejected my good intentions along with my gift.

I'd accepted her apology eventually, despite my hurt feelings—those slippers had been very carefully chosen for their warmth and rich design, and I'd have loved for somebody to give *me* a pair—but I'd noticed since that she'd never worn them.

Until now. Which was about as clear an indication of her mental state as you could ask for.

I persuaded her that she wasn't going anywhere for a while, got her into the kitchen and fed her what was surely her first food of the day. Then I parked her in front of the TV and I checked out the telephone answering machine. My one hope was that Gran had called.

She hadn't. Several irate or puzzled authors had—clients of my mom's—and her lawyer, and some friends wanting to know how things were going. That was all. I decided I would call Mom's office in the morning, in case Gran had tried to contact me there.

I sat up most of the night in Mom's room, watching her sleep and watching TV and dozing off myself, but not for long.

Having failed to locate Gran, I could see only one way left for me to go: to tackle Brightner directly. Myself. Of course if I did, I might never see my mom, waking or sleeping, zombie or alive, again. On the other hand, that was a sure thing if I did nothing at all.

So next morning I ate as much Grape Nuts as I could get down, spooned some into Mom, and headed for school early. Which gave me a chance to hang around by myself, cold and scared, while some of the boys played with a football in the street and girls stood in little knots gossiping and giggling. For all I had in common with any of them today—including my friend Megan, who only came early to watch her latest crush pass the football—I might have been a Martian.

I kind of wished I'd come late rather than early; except that watching Mom pad around in the despised carpet slippers was too awful. My only comfort was the silver glove, which I wore.

I handed in a forged note from my mom for my missed Monday and ghosted through my morning classes with only one thing on my mind: did I really dare walk into Brightner's office and demand my mom's reflection back?

At lunch, Barb sat down with me. "You get home all right? You should have heard the fuss that weirdo made! My mom couldn't figure out what it was all about. She finally threatened to call the building security man, it being way past closing time by then anyhow. You got all that stuff I lent you?"

I handed over the borrowed clothes. Barb gave me a neat package in return. "Here's yours. I threw it all in the washer last night when I got home. Smells like curry in there now."

"Barb," I said, "you're great."

Barb said, "What now?" She looked at the glove on my hand and raised her eyebrows. "Going to see somebody?" she said.

"Going to try," I said.

"I'd keep you company," she said, looking away from me, "but I can't. Brother's in real trouble. So my mother's busy, but there's a big buyer coming in today. I got to go mind the store soon as I finish lunch."

"That's okay," I said, with a sinking heart.

"You know I'd come with you," she said, kind of hot and proud. "I *would*. But Brother—"

"Don't apologize, it's okay," I said, wishing hard that I had a brother or a sister to help me, even a brother or sister who kept getting into serious hot water and disrupting my life.

"Who's apologizing?" Barb snapped.

Lennie walked by. I called him, thinking maybe I could ask him to hang around in the hall outside Brightner's office when I went in there, as a sort of witness, I guess.

He stopped by our table but didn't sit down. "How you doing?" he said in a funny, stiff way.

"I could use a favor," I said.

He shrugged and looked away. "I could have used one yesterday. So long. Some guys are waiting for me."

And he walked away. If anybody was waiting for him, I didn't see them.

It's amazing how even in the midst of the greatest crisis of your life, a thing like that can hurt your feelings. "What's the matter with him?" I said indignantly.

Barb gave me a look. "*Somebody* was supposed to read something of his in English class yesterday, remember? Only *somebody* didn't show up, and Lennie had to read it himself. The way I hear it, it was not a raving success, and he threw up afterward in the boys' room. Nerves, you know? Some people are real sensitive that way."

"Oh, God." I groaned. "I was locked in the spice pantry by an Indian witch at the time! How in the heck can I ever explain that?"

Barb patted my shoulder and got up. "You're smart, you'll work it out. Listen, I gotta go. Call me, okay? At the store. I want to know what happens. And you can hide out there again if you need to."

But we both knew I wouldn't, not now that Ushah knew about The Makeup Stop.

"Hey," she added. "You got that little mirror I gave you?"

I did, tucked away in my shirt pocket, with the flap buttoned for security. "You need it back?" I said.

"Nope. Just keep it by you."

She left. I sat there alone, wondering if anybody could help me. No use even asking Megan. And who else was there? Just me, dumb and desperate on the fringes of crazy things I didn't understand and couldn't expect anybody else to jump into with me.

So: I might as well go after the Demon Shrink at sixth period, when, according to the schedule posted on his office door, he was free. Who could tell, maybe the silver glove would fly off my hand and dive down his throat and choke him while he was busy laughing at me!

Right after lunch I saw him in the hall talking with one

of the science teachers. He saw me, too, and he didn't so much as blink, just went on chatting with Miss Bell. Flirting, if you can believe that! I believed it, and from the look on Miss Bell's face she believed it too, and didn't mind a bit.

Maybe he had his eye on another "bride."

The trouble with deciding definitely when you're going to do something is that the time comes. On the way to my doom I stopped to take a drink at the fountain in the fourth-floor hallway, which gave me a chance to see if *anybody* was around. Who knew what kind of trap Brightner might have set for me?

Here came Mrs. Denby, tick-ticking down the hallway from the assistant principal's office in her high heels with an armload of files. I winced. My feet still ached from yesterday. I would never feel the same way about high heels again.

"Hi, Mrs. Denby," I said loudly, and she blinked and sort of shook her head—looking for my name in it among all the others, probably—and said, "Oh, hello, Valentine."

Not the person I would have chosen to be the last one to see me before I stepped into the monster's lair, but she would have to do.

I clenched my hand in the silver glove and knocked on Brightner's door.

"Come in, Tina," he called from inside. Reading my mind again! Or at least sensing my presence before he saw me. I choked down my fear, concentrating instead on pure indignation at being called by my baby-name, and I walked into his office.

There he sat, leaning back in the beat-up swivel chair with his hands behind his head. Mr. Casual. On a cleared place on the scarred oak desk, a smouldering cigar butt was parked in a glass ashtray shaped like a pear.

"Hi," he said. "I thought I saw trouble in your face when I was talking to Miss Bell. What's up? Tell me about it. I'm the guy to talk to."

He absolutely took my breath away, coming on all solicitous like that. After everything that had happened! Funny, though—I hadn't noticed before: he had warm brown eyes in his rather silly, sympathetic hound-dog face.

All of a sudden I felt so funny and confused that I knew I had to get down to business fast, while I still had some idea of what I'd come in here for.

"My mom went ice-skating with you on Saturday night," I challenged.

"Is that what you think she did?" he said, reaching for the cigar butt and taking a good puff at it.

"She *did*. And she came back weird." I meant this to be an accusation that would jar the truth out of him. It came out weak and childish.

He nodded at the chair facing him across the desk. "Sit down, Tina."

With the door open behind me, what could happen? I felt dizzy. I sat.

He lounged on his side of the desk like a comfy old walrus, tapping ash into the glass pear. "Do you think if your mom goes out it means she doesn't care about you?"

"No." If there's one thing I can't stand, it's people who have a system to explain everything a kid does or says, even if a particular kid happens to be acting and speaking out of their own life and not anybody's system. When my mom went out, what it meant to me was that she was living her own life, which was fine with me. If she lived hers, then I had a good argument for living mine. Besides, going out made her feel good, and when she felt good she was a lot nicer to live with.

I was not about to go into any of that with the Demon Shrink. Since he was so smart, let him guess.

Not him. He cruised right on with his theories. "Is it like when your father left? Do you think it's all your fault? Did you think your family broke up on account of something you did?"

"I never thought that about my father," I said, confused. Did I ever think that? No, I told myself fiercely, don't let him distract you with this junk!

He said, "I imagine there's some conflict for you about your mother's, ah, social life. Here she is telling you to stop and go at the same time about boys, since of course she wants to be sure that you learn how to handle yourself with them but not get in too deep for your age. But for her, it's all go, right? It would be, for an attractive woman like that."

"Don't talk like that about my mother," I croaked. There was something incredibly nasty about the way he was just strolling around in what he imagined my life with my mom to be like.

And I sure did not want to have him sit there and discuss how attractive he thought my mother was, which felt like an icky sort of intrusion into Mom's private life. I had expected to be scared, but this guy was also making me feel a little sick.

He smiled. "Have some candy," he said, edging the dish toward me across the desk. "It's just fennel seeds coated in sugar and food coloring. A little sugar wouldn't hurt you, you look washed out."

Never take candy from strangers, my mom had always said. My poor mom.

"You've got her reflection," I said, bringing the conversation back to basics. "She's hardly a person at all now. And all those other people's shadows—what are you trying to do, anyway?"

"I thought you didn't want me to talk about her."

"That's not what I said," I muttered woozily.

He studied me a minute. Then he leaned across the desk and spoke quietly to me, seriously. "Your mother's safe. Couldn't you tell that when you saw her skating with me? That's why I showed her to you. She's safe and she's happy."

"You're lying!" I said. Now we were on the subject, and that was the best I could do!

"You saw her," he insisted calmly. "She was smiling, wasn't she? Think back. How did she look?"

"It doesn't matter how she looked! You put a spell on her, that's all. She doesn't know what she's doing."

He pursed up his lips as if he was really considering what I'd said. "I'm sure a smart kid like you knows," he remarked, "that it's very common for a child of divorced parents to have all sorts of fantasies about any man who seems likely to replace her real dad."

A wave of dizziness washed over me. I shook it off. I said, "That's a lot of crap and you know it!"

"Is it?" he said mildly.

"Tell me how many kids like that make up fantasies about people's shadows being stolen—old people, street people, for cripes' sake—people who could disappear and everybody would say, oh, that's too bad, but of course it happens!"

"Disappear?" he said, with this lazy smile that made me twist inside. "Who said anything about disappearing?"

"Then what is going to happen to them?" I said.

"Something fine and grand," he said expansively. "A new life. A fresh start in a new place. Isn't that the American ideal?"

"What?" I said, bewildered. "What good is a fresh start to a bunch of old people and bums?"

"Oh, not their worn-out bodies," he said, flipping one thick paw in the air to dismiss this worthless notion. "Surely your grandmother figured this out and told you? I'm only taking spirits, souls, which I'm going to install in new bodies. Strong, new bodies; strong and young."

That was the kind of thing necromancers do, Gran had said. "And dead," I whispered. "*Dead* bodies, right?"

"Clever girl," he smiled. "Right at the moment, yes. But not for much longer. That's the whole idea."

"Whose dead bodies? Where?"

"All right, I'll play," he said, fishing a fresh cigar out of his breast pocket and clipping off one end with a little silver clipper. "Suppose there was a war going on, somewhere else, somewhere *far*."

A war, Gran had said, taking up all the energies of Sorcery Hall.

"And suppose one side had a lot of casualties and was

103

running out of recruits. That side might hire a very talented recruiter to go and find some new fighters. The very talented recruiter could be somebody who knew how to patch up dead warriors, bodies that have fighting strength and skill built into their nerve-paths and muscles and that aren't actually used up yet, just—damaged. Suppose he could get them up and moving around again, using souls lifted out of other bodies—old bodies, sick and crazy bodies."

"You can't," I said, feeling a little sick and crazy myself.

"Who said anything about me?" he said, shooting his eyebrows high in surprise. He lit the fresh cigar. "I'm talking about a figure out of fantasy, a wizard from a role-playing game. I'm talking about the greatest necromancer ever seen. *That* person could do it. You bet he could."

I swallowed, thinking of Dirty Rose. "They wouldn't fight," I said. "Street people won't fight in anybody's stupid war!"

"Sure they will." He actually chuckled. I have never heard such an evil sound in my life. "I'll fix the major kinks in their miserable minds. They'll wake up scared to death and totally disoriented in their new bodies, and they'll be hustled into battle first thing. The bodies, warrior-bodies, will know what to do automatically. Fear will do the rest. Men-souls, women-souls, it makes no difference—fear makes hard fighters. They'll fight so well that I'm sure this recruiter I'm talking about will get a contract for a return trip. There are lots of souls here on your pretty earth, enough to man even a big, long war."

He's really saying this, I thought, with Mrs. Denby's footsteps clicking by in the hall outside, as they did just then. But why not? If she did happen to overhear what he was saying, she'd probably think it was just some weird kind of therapy going on in the office of the new school shrink.

"And we're left with what?" I said. "Their bodies? A whole bunch of people keeling over dead all of a sudden?"

He shrugged. "So what? Think of it as a favor. This planet is wildly overpopulated."

"You really stink, you know that?" I squalled.

He made a tsk-tsk sound. "Your mother said you read a lot. Do you always get so worked up over a mere story?"

"My mom's no—no warrior," I said. Against my wobbling will, my eyes filled with hot tears.

"Oh, there'll be no zombie-battlefield for her, don't worry about that." He sipped smoke from the cigar and his expression became bland. "You may find this hard to believe, Tina," he purred, "but I'm very fond of your mother, and she knows it. Or to put it another way, she's something very special and I know it. She has great potential, which I know how to put to use, if she'll let me; and she will. She's smart enough to know what a terrific team we could make, the two of us . . . I don't really need a fetch in her case. I only made one, a very special one made of light instead of shadow, as a form of basic insurance. She'd come with me willingly without it."

"Oh, yeah?" I said. "Well, how about Ushah?"

"Ushah," he said, taking another puff and waving smoke away, "is a silly, primitive woman. She gets wild ideas. It's your mother I want for my wife."

"You have a wife!" I yelled. "Lots of wives! Ushah told me! You're some kind of lousy rotten Bluebeard!"

"Calm down," he said. "You don't really know what you're getting all excited about. A young kid like you, even a very bright young kid with a very smart grandmother, shouldn't mess around in things she doesn't understand."

I jumped up and stood there weaving and glaring, hanging onto the edge of Brightner's desk, my throat all dry from blue cigar smoke. "We'll stop you," I said. "Gran and me and—and Sorcery Hall!"

"Sorcery Hall?" He grinned. "No, Tina, not Sorcery Hall. This is their war we've been talking about, those know-it-alls! They're much too busy defending themselves to even notice a little scuffle like this, let alone divert any of their own forces to try to influence its outcome. You're on your own in this one, you and the old lady. Against *me*."

He paused to let that sink in. Then he said, "It would be better, much better, for you to stop struggling and give in. You could start by bringing your grandmother to me tonight. I'm willing to take the three of you into my household. You could all be together. There would be great advantages."

He leaned toward me, talking in a gruff, wheedling tone, smiling at me with his dark, hound-dog eyes.

"Do you want your mother to be happy? She would be, with me. Do you want your Gran to live a long, long time, maybe forever? I could arrange it. Do you want to practice magic yourself? I could teach you."

"Leave me alone," I said, or anyway I tried to say it.

"I think we need to negotiate," he said. "But to talk properly with a fellow like me, you have to descend to my level. I'm a plain man, from plain people, remember? You and I should start over, with the basics. Such as an old-fashioned handshake. With the left hand. I'm a lefty myself, didn't you notice? But not with a glove on, that would be an insult.

"So you'll have to take the glove off, won't you."

I actually took hold of one finger and began to pull off the glove. The cigar smoke had to be a drug, eating up my willpower and turning me all around.

I had to get out of there. I turned hazily and lurched in what I hoped frantically was the direction of the door.

He said, "Think about it. You have till closing time."

I stopped, rocking on my feet. "What do you mean by that?" My voice sounded far away in my own ears.

He said, "Tonight I expect to fill out my initial draft of recruits. I'll be leaving. With your mother, of course. Definitely with your mother."

"Closing time," I said. "What's closing time?"

"Think about it a little. Clever kid like you, you'll figure it out."

As I stumbled out of his office, he called after me, "I'll be watching for you. You're a real scrapper, I can see that. We'll take off the *gloves*, right? And really settle this, once and for all."

13
In the Bag

No way could I just waltz back into a classroom after that. I hid out for a little while in the girls' room, slapping cold water on my face with my right hand—I didn't plan to ever take the silver glove off again—and blinking at my face in the mirror. To look at me, you would never guess what I had just been through. Just let me try and tell anybody about that crazy conversation, and see where it got me!

After a while I picked up my bookbag and walked out of the school building. Maybe I would never see it, or my friends, or anything of that whole life again. I had no idea what to do now. None. There's a point, I guess, when you realize that what you're up against is just too much for you; that you are done for.

Done-for is how I felt, but how could that be, when I was only fighting for what was right? My mom, our lives, people's *souls*, for cripes' sake? We were right, and we were going to lose, because I was outclassed, outgunned, stymied. It was just me and Brightner now, in a little peripheral squabble while Sorcery Hall was busy with the main show, the wizard war.

Brightner knew he was way too much for me. I believed it, too. Why not? Just because I had managed not to get snagged by The Claw—so far? What a record!

With this bitter thought thudding around and around in my head I trudged home, not looking left or right for fear of seeing some poor jerk walk by without a shadow—some jerk I couldn't do a thing to help.

I let myself into the apartment and checked on Mom. She was asleep on the living room rug with the shawl collar of her robe hiked up over her head. Then I went downstairs into the basement to do the laundry.

I suppose that sounds funny, but when you're all used up and sort of drizzling drearily inside instead of thinking, but your body is buzzing and twitching with the energy of fear, a routine mindless task is just right. The kind of thing that normally you try to get out of doing.

Mom and I always took turns doing the laundry. She actually liked it, because down in the basement with the machines grinding around and around she could sit and read manuscripts without being interrupted by the telephone.

I generally hated the basement because it was creepy. Today nothing could scare me, not after my session with the Demon Shrink.

So after I checked the phone messages—including three solicitations from computers trying to sell insurance—I emptied the hamper. I sorted the stuff out (there wasn't much; neither of us had been exactly going through our wardrobes lately) and lugged it all, with soap powder and some leftovers to nibble on while I waited and *The Count of Monte Cristo* to read, down in the elevator.

The basement is warm in cold weather, from the boilers. The walls are painted with green and yellow enamel to make the basement cheerful, I guess, which it isn't. You have to

108

walk past the wire cages of the storage room to get to the machines, for one thing.

I have always thought the storage area was incredibly sinister. Who knew what might be lurking in there in all that piled-up junk, watching you through the wire mesh? Things strong enough to break any of the assortment of padlocks on the doors, you can bet. Going by there was always good for a thrill.

Not that afternoon. I plodded on into the wash room without a stir of apprehension. I guess I was all terrified out.

The wash room is like a laundromat, with one row of washers down the middle, three dryers in a row at the end of the room, two tables for folding that people are always fighting over, and a set of molded plastic chairs in bright orange. Nests of pipes wind along the ceiling and the corners of the room, and huge black hoses snake into a row of sinks behind the washers, to drain the wash water. The floor is covered with linoleum tile.

The room was still and dim, the machines were silent. I switched on the fluorescent lights and got to work.

Most days people's hired houseworkers come down with washes to do, which is okay, except that sometimes they bring noisy radios or they smoke up the place so you can hardly breathe. There are bright-colored tin ashtrays with scalloped edges all over the place. Whenever I'm down there I try to sneak a few of them out with me and throw them away, as a subtle form of discouragement.

So I was glad to have the place to myself. I couldn't even get into *Monte Cristo*, though Edmund Dantes was just about to take his revenge on rotten Danglars, which is a part of the book I particularly like.

I had a lot to think about. Too much. Not all of it terrible, though. In fact, I could see some ways in which the visit to Brightner hadn't been a total loss. I knew now that the glove did protect me from Brightner himself, at least in some ways and in some circumstances—unless he had been only pretending, misleading me so that later on I would trust the powers of the glove when it couldn't save me.

Not too likely. Why not gobble me right then and there while he had the chance, if he could? I didn't think he was the kind to put off till tomorrow anything he could gulp down today.

And I knew that he didn't have any more idea where Gran was than I did.

If only I'd had the nerve—the presence of mind—whatever it took to just punch him in the middle of his smirking puss with the silver glove! Maybe that would have done some good, maybe he would have disappeared in a puff of smoke (so why hadn't Gran done that? She was the one with the magic here, not dumb old me).

But once I'd chewed all that over a few times, my mind pulled me back inexorably to the broader situation, which was awful. There was no comfort in it whatever.

This was the last day of my normal life. That night, somehow, I would have to try to keep Mom from going with her reflection-fetch, and I would probably lose that struggle. There was no telling what would happen to me, or to her, let alone what had happened to my Gran.

Now I knew what Brightner was. All that talk about great wizards and necromancy—he was here to shanghai innocent people into somebody else's horrible war. He was a slave dealer, and his victims were all doomed to die in some far-off battle. They were sacrifices.

As for my mom's "special" place in his schemes, the idea of Brightner taking her away forever made my whole mind fly apart.

I sat there in the hot wash room with the book open in my lap, holding the same page with my gloved left hand, thinking very un-urgently about eating the stale end of salami I'd brought to nibble on. I stared at the machines—bright colors swirling around in the cold wash, pale ones in the hot—and my thoughts flopped around getting nowhere the same way.

Then William walked in. "Hi," he said. "Thought I heard somebody in here."

I said, "Hi, William."

William was the new handyman for the building. He could fix anything, which is why nobody wanted him fired even though it was rumored that he drank.

He was a tall, gloomy-looking man in khaki work clothes and big yellow boots. He talked slowly and not much, and had the dirtiest hands I have ever seen. The kids in the building had decided that he probably just gave up washing them, considering the number of greasy grubby jobs he had to do every day fixing pipes and wires and locks in people's apartments.

He stood in the doorway gazing somberly at me. "Got something to show you, if you want to see. She come in this morning early, poor little thing."

"She?" I said. "Who?"

"Come look."

So I left the book and the laundry and followed William to one of the utility closets. He opened it cautiously, not very wide. "Just take a quick look," he said. "She's real shy, real wild."

From the deepest, darkest corner of the utility closet, wide yellow eyes glared out at us. I heard a faint, dry hiss that ended in a string of minute coughs, like miniature explosions.

"What is it," I said dully, not caring, really, "a cat?"

William nodded and shut the door again. "Stray," he said. "Found her in the boiler room this morning, sleeping near the warmth. Cold night last night."

A cat. Something stirred in my mind, a breath of something: thought, hope, a rising edge of eager curiosity. A cat! Ushah, swinging a mop at a gray streak in Kali's Kitchen—

"What's she look like, William?"

He shrugged. "Not much. Little gray cat, kinda old I think, little bit old and slow or I couldn't of caught her."

"What are you going to do with her?"

111

"Feed her up, maybe take her home when she calms down," he said slowly. He looked consideringly at me. " 'Less you'd like to take her. Don't think your mom would like it, though. A stray and all."

Right at that time my mom wouldn't have minded if I'd brought home a nine-hundred-pound yak, but I wasn't going to go into that. So I thanked him for showing me the cat, and then I watched him lope off to the elevators with his toolbox.

Then I opened the utility closet, and the cat shot out past my ankles and disappeared into the storage area.

Great. Good work, Val.

I don't have much experience with pets. Don't get me wrong: I like cats. I love cats. But I am a city kid, and pets are not taken for granted here.

I once convinced my mom to let me have a kitten from a litter in an apartment upstairs, on trial. So far, so good. Then I blew the whole thing. The same night that I brought the kitten into our apartment, my mom found me in the bathroom at eleven o'clock, bright red in the face, coughing and wheezing and throwing up. Obviously, she deduced, I was allergic to cats. The kitten would have to go back.

I screamed and I cried and I denied over and over that I was allergic, making myself even sicker and more miserable. Mom, very sensibly, locked the kitten in the pantry and next morning she gave it back to the people upstairs. And that was the end of my pet-owning days.

What had actually happened—and you'll see why I couldn't tell my mom this—was that when I took the kitten to bed with me that night it began crying for its mother and the other kittens. I wanted to comfort it. Logically, to make it feel at home, I figured I should treat it as its cat mother would.

So I'd been licking the kitten's fur, and of course I'd swallowed some. I defy you to show me any kid who won't have an allergic reaction to actually eating a cat's fur.

I went back into the wash room and sat down again, wondering how to recapture William's gray cat. How could I lure her back? With salami, of course! Cats love salty meats, everybody knows that!

Having no knife with me, I bit the salami end into little pieces and put them down on the floor, making a salami trail from the doorway. Then I opened my book and pretended to read.

What with the machines churning along and Danglars getting his comeuppance, which he richly deserved, I didn't know the cat was there until it sneezed a small, neat cat-sneeze from somewhere close by.

I glanced at it out of the corner of my eye, holding very still.

The cat crouched by the wall only a few yards from me. All but the last two bits of salami were gone. She was watching me and licking her chops with her narrow pink tongue.

This was my first real look at her, and she wasn't much: just what William had said, small and bony, the color of the dust that gathers underneath furniture, with a torn ear and a bald spot over one hip and a kink in the end of her tail as if somebody had slammed a door on it once.

She darted forward, grabbed a morsel of salami with a right hook, and retreated again.

I sat like a statue, hardly breathing, and when the cat came for the last and nearest salami-bite, I made a grab for her, leading with the gloved hand, which at least had some protection.

As soon as I touched her—I am pretty fast—she let out a yowl in the midst of which I heard, with heart-stopping clarity, words, words uttered in a thin, distorted version of my grandmother's voice!

"Hang on, Valentine, don't let go!"

A wild, brief struggle followed. Somehow I stuffed the poor cat, kicking and writhing, into the smallest of the laundry bags, the white cotton one, and I yanked the draw-string tight.

The bag leaped and lumped around on the floor while I

113

sort of danced around it, sucking my finger where one flailing set of claws had connected, and yelling, "Gran! Gran! Is that you?" like a lunatic. As I said, it was very lucky that nobody else was washing clothes in the basement that afternoon.

Finally the bag got quiet and the small voice panted, "Heavens, what a dustup! Thank goodness I've finally found you, Val! Are you all right? Not scratched to pieces, I hope?"

I crouched down to talk to the bag, not daring to touch it. "I'm fine, I'm fine! Gran! That was you at Kali's Kitchen, wasn't it? What happened?"

"I went there with Rose, as planned," said the breathless voice of Gran-the-cat, "disguised as the street person I might well be, in other circumstances. Seeing Ushah there threw me off balance, so to speak—"

"Ushah!" I said. "You talk as if you know her!"

"I do," said the voice in the bag. "Or I did. She was a wild talent, like me, but she dropped out of Sorcery Hall. Didn't care for the discipline, charged off on her own, and now look at her! She didn't recognize me, of course. She doesn't pay attention to other women at all unless they're potential rivals. But I was so surprised that I did something very foolish: I ate some enchanted food there."

"Gran!" I cried.

The bag surged slightly and settled again. "Well, yes; but I was hungry, and Rose handed me a little dish of colored candies, and before I knew what I was doing, I popped some into my mouth.

"Well, my own powers were roused up to protect me at once, of course, but the best I could manage under the circumstances was to switch forms, and at that only into some creature analogous to the sort of human being I appeared to be. So—stray old street-woman into stray old alley cat, I'm afraid."

I said, "You mean there's no cat, really—this is you?"

"For the time being," she said. "Very awkward, too. There I was in Kali's Kitchen and I couldn't get out because

114

this little cat-brain was so crazed with fear that it was impossible to direct. I kept having this irresistible urge to hide when I should have been escaping, you see. While I'm in cat form, to some extent I'm stuck with cat limitations, and they are considerable."

I said, "But you got away."

The voice said, "By luck. It was lucky for me, lovie, that you ignored my instructions! In her eagerness to get her hands on you, Ushah left the side door open, so I was able to slip out and make my way up here in search of you; and that's been an adventure, I can tell you. But I won't, not at the moment."

This is embarrassing to admit, but I was crying with relief. I sort of blubbered and gulped while I talked. "Oh, Gran, listen—he's taking them tonight, all the captive souls, and Mom, too!" And I told her all.

The bag lay still, mounded in a neat, small-cat shape and pointed over the ears. Gran said, "So, it's as bad as I thought; he's built your mother into his scheme, he's using her to fuel a very grand structure of evil magic indeed! Well, we have a chance, then. Using her powers, perhaps he's overreached himself, lovie. He might not be able to make it work on his own. If we can win her back from him, the whole structure may come apart. So we do have a chance. Though it's not a very good one, to tell the truth, and if we fail—"

"If we fail, what?" I said.

Gran said slowly, "He'll try to take us as well, you and me, Val—to capture the rest of our family talent for his own uses. We mustn't let that happen! We must break his spell. Somehow."

She sighed a sigh that turned into a cat-yawn that lifted the bag and sucked in the cloth a little.

"Easier said than done," she went on briskly. "Never mind, we must do what we can. To start with, lovie, you can take me upstairs with you just as I am, here in this bag. If I get away from you again, I don't know that I'll be able to make my way back, being so subject to cat-fears while I'm cat-formed."

"But why don't you just change back into your own shape?" I said. A horrible explanation occurred to me. "You're not—not *stuck* like this, are you?"

"No, not now that you've touched me with the silver glove," came Gran's voice. "It's a great unlocker and tugger-loose, is the silver glove. But transformations are exhausting. I'll need everything I've got and then some before this night is out. Besides, I do have a use for this shape still. I think I'll keep it for a bit, limitations and all."

"I wish you'd, you know, come *back*, Gran," I moaned.

"Don't cry, lovie. We've done rather well, between us. Thanks to you, I slipped right out of his clutches, didn't I? Ushah is in for it if he finds out."

"It's true," I said, feeling more cheerful. "He has no idea where you are. Or, um, what you are, either."

"Good thing Brightner himself wasn't supervising things at the restaurant," Gran said with satisfaction. "That's the weakness of bad guys, have you noticed? Overreaching. Greediness. He does have all those other collection points to attend to, after all— like the 'clinic' in Buffalo. No wonder he needs an assistant! He's such a busy fellow, with shadows to gather here and in Buffalo and perhaps other places as well. Not to mention the time he's taken off romancing your poor silly mother!"

Gloom invaded me. "You know all about that?"

"Indeed I do," the cat said. "You did your best to protect her. No use blaming yourself, lovie."

"Well, I won't," I said. "If we can get Mom *back*."

"Her, and the others, poor things," said Gran's voice. The neck of the bag twitched slightly as the cat pawed delicately at it from inside. "We must stop the necromancer if we can."

"If!" I said. "But you studied in Sorcery Hall, and he's just a—a renegade. He can't have more power than you do!"

"I am old, lovie. I don't know how this will come out.

116

We will try, though, won't we? We must. And we have a deadline."

My heart began to pound.

"Closing time," I said. "At Kali's Kitchen, I guess. Closing time tonight. He was telling the truth about that, wasn't he—not just trying to scare me?"

"Oh yes," Gran-the-cat said. "He told you his intentions, and you'd be a fool not to be scared."

Well, I wasn't a fool and I sure was scared. I stood up and paced around, glaring at the quiet machines. "But even if we miss the deadline, you could find out where he took her. We could go after her and get her back!"

"Not likely, lovie," Gran said after a moment, shifting uneasily inside the cotton bag. "The longer she's with him, the more like poor Ushah she'll become—obedient, I mean. To him."

"Poor Ushah, nothing!" I growled. "She tried to *get* me!"

"Yes, poor Ushah!" Gran said firmly. "Being under Brightner's influence has made her into her own worst self. Remember, like all powerful people gone bad he uses fear and lies to corrupt and control others. He's made Ushah afraid of her own strength and afraid of being without him. That's his magic hold on her. Believing his lies, she's become his creature and lost herself.

"He'll do the same with your mother, and I'm afraid she's not very well prepared to resist him. You might follow her only to find her unwilling to leave him."

The idea of my mom, who had pulled herself together after her divorce and made herself a career and everything, who was an important person to a whole bunch of writers and editors, becoming a willing captive of stinking Brightner was absolutely crazy-making. I didn't know whether to cry or scream.

"What are we going to do?" I said. "Gran, just tell me. I'll try anything!"

"I would start," said the cat mildly, "by getting the laundry out of the machines."

117

14
The Witch's Daughter

When I got back with the laundry and the cat, I found Mom sitting on the fire stairs on our landing, brushing her hair with languid strokes. She was still in her bathrobe and carpet slippers.

And she looked—well, at first sight she looked like a nightmare. She had obviously been busy in front of her dressing table mirror putting on makeup now and then while I'd been down in the basement. There was makeup on top of makeup: crusted mascara sticking her eyelashes together, flaking layers of liquid foundation and powder, lipstick caked all over her mouth and smeared on her front teeth. She was a parody of what Barb had made of me to help me escape from Ushah and The Claw.

When I asked her what she was doing there, she said, "It's late." For a second there I was electrified by the hope that somehow she had recovered, escaped Brightner on her own, and was her old self again, checking up on her errant daughter.

No such luck. The next second she frowned vaguely and added, "We're supposed to leave soon."

My hope went flat and left me feeling more tired and discouraged than before.

I got her and the laundry into the apartment. Gran instructed me to leave the white laundry bag, open, on my bed, so that she could venture out when her cat-nerves recovered from the petrifying elevator ride up from the basement.

Meanwhile I made Mom some soup and toast and nagged her into eating it (I don't think she'd had a meal all day) and cleaned her up. She let me scrub her face for her with the washrag, as if she were a little kid. It was horrible.

Gran-the-cat watched, huge-eyed and trembling in the doorway of the bedroom. That was as close to us as she could bring herself, since her cat-nerves certainly hadn't been helped by the ride upstairs in the white laundry bag. But she could talk to me from there, and she did.

Gran's theory was that when Brightner took off tonight, of all his victims Mom was the only one whose actual present *body* would be fetched rather than discarded (translation, left mysteriously dead). In Mom's case, Brightner wanted the whole package, body and soul. And he would send Mom's reflection to fetch it.

Since we had to be at Kali's Kitchen around closing time to confront Brightner, we couldn't stick around the apartment to try to hold Mom back. But Gran said there was a small chance that knocking Mom out a little with sleeping pills might at least slow down her response, if it didn't stop her. Any unexpected turn of events such as a delay could work for us against Brightner. He was the one with the plans. We were more or less improvising, which left us more flexible than he was. We hoped.

Not that I hoped much. I mean, think of it—a kid and

an old alley cat, against Brightner, Ushah the Foul, and The Claw!

We were probably crazy, but I didn't feel the awful hopelessness I had before, maybe because I had Gran back, sort of. Or maybe what kept me going was rage about this parody of my mom that Brightner had palmed off on me.

Which is how I came to be sitting with my mom that evening, coaxing her to drink down a glass of warm milk with two of her sleeping pills dissolved in it. Too bad I couldn't take a pill myself. Prospects of a totally terrifying night stretched ahead.

"Swallow," I told Mom. "Come on, drink some more."

In the doorway, Gran said, "Oh, damn," and whirled around and bit at her haunch.

I stared, fascinated.

Gran looked wearily up at me again. Her voice came out slightly hoarse. "You have no idea—these little beasties have such a limited number of actions open to them! When something presses my buttons, like an itch that might be a fleabite, the whole organism responds willy-nilly. *And* I've got a bad case of worms."

In a way, I think I preferred having the cat talk to me from the bag. The way its lips twisted to make the consonants was weird—a kind of insane-looking snarling, something like bad animation in a cartoon. A pity Barb, with her Thundercats mania, wasn't here to see this!

"But not Alzheimer's, right?" I said. "Cats can't get that, can they?"

"I don't know," Gran said.

"Though actually, if anybody around here is acting like an Alzheimer's victim, it's Mom, not you!"

If you think a cat talking to you is rough, try a cat laughing. It was positively grotesque.

Mom drank most of the doped milk with me holding both her hands curled around the warm glass. Then she pushed me away, sat up, and craned her neck, looking

120

around for something. "Hairbrush," she said. "Where did I leave it? I can't go looking like this."

I pushed her back against the pillows. "For Pete's sake," I shouted, "if you do any more brushing you'll brush yourself bald! You want to be bald?"

She let me feed her a few more swallows of spiked milk before she turned her face away and burrowed down under the covers like an overtired kid.

Gran-the-cat said from the doorway. "All right, lovie, I think she'll stay put. Pour the rest of the milk out in a saucer and put it on the floor for me, would you?"

"This stuff is doped," I reminded her. "I'll get you some fresh milk."

"No," she said. "That's the milk I want. We have to wait now, till closing time; and my poor little cat-body needs some rest after so much excitement. Also, I'll have to be very quiet while getting past Ushah tonight, and maybe past Brightner himself."

"Great," I said, "but suppose that milk knocks you out cold? How can I wake you when the time comes?"

"You won't have to," Gran said. "Don't worry."

Fine. My real worry about the sleeping pills went much deeper. Not knowing how much of the dissolved stuff was left in the remaining milk, let alone how much of it was safe to feed to a cat—if any!—worried me a lot. "But, Gran—"

"Good heavens, I thought all you young people nowadays were as easy as your corner pharmacist with all sorts of 'substances,' as they call such things! This is not the time to get fussy about drugs."

I felt my cheeks heat up. I mean, I've tried a few things, but it would have been embarrassing to admit just how ignorant and inexperienced I really was about stuff that some kids could synthesize with a chem set. I stayed with the heart of the problem. "But you could—I mean, a cat could die of sleeping pills, couldn't it?"

"Oh, for heaven's sake," Gran said with weary impatience, "this rackety little puss-heart can only take so much

121

more excitement as it is, child! In my opinion, we're better off with the risk of overdosing."

I stood there gripping the warm glass. "Change back," I begged. "Please, Gran!"

"Not till I have to, I've told you." Gran-the-cat's eyelids drooped shut. Her scratchy cat-voice murmured, "I'm sorry, lovie. It's a hard choice. But think of what we stand to lose . . ."

"I hate this!" I moaned to myself. "I hate it!"

But I did it.

Some milk splashed on the kitchen floor because my hands were shaking when I poured. I put the saucer down and went out in the hall to wait, so I wouldn't make the cat more nervous by hanging over it. After a long time, I heard tiny lapping sounds.

Then silence; and then a small thud. I bounded back into the kitchen, my insides clenched in expectation of the worst.

The cat lay on its side. Its knobby little body was slack and still, and kneeling for a closer look I saw a sliver of pale eyeball between partly closed eyelids. But the scrawny flanks rose and fell and one forepaw twitched slightly. I groaned with relief.

Then I went back to Mom's bedroom. I turned the TV on—some cop show—with the sound way down. I just wanted the comfort of the flashing pictures while I waited.

The phone rang. I almost fell off the bed, grabbing for it fast so the noise wouldn't rouse Mom. A girl from my history class wanted to check the assignment for tomorrow. I went into my own room and looked it up for her, thinking, when was the last time I did any homework? If I survived Brightner, would I be able to survive my teachers at school?

When I'd finished giving the information and hung up, I found Mom lying on her side and looking at me.

"Mom?" I said. "Go back to sleep."

"Hi, darling," she said and yawned. "What time is it?"

"*Late,*" I said, tucking her in firmly all over again. What was I going to do if she didn't go back to sleep, give her more pills? I didn't dare.

"Never too late," she murmured, smiling. "Some day my prince will come." She began humming the song from the Walt Disney cartoon movie. My Mom thought she was Snow White going under an enchanted sleep. Only it was the Demon Shrink, not the handsome prince, who meant to wake her. And there wouldn't be any happily-ever-after, not with his string of wives and his awful recruiting "contracts," not to mention Ushah the Ghastly.

"Go to sleep," I said.

She hummed, ignoring me.

I had an inspiration. I snuggled down next to her on the bedspread. "Mom," I said, "I can't sleep. Tell me a story."

She had often dozed off while telling me bedtime stories when I was little. Now she sighed and was still for a little. I thought maybe her mind was wandering so widely that she hadn't even heard me.

Then she said softly, "Once there was a witch, and she had a daughter."

She started to tell me about a witch from Scotland who married a baker in New York, and their daughter; in other words, about herself and Gran. She frowned woozily and her fingers pulled and plucked at the tufted knots on her bedspread as she told me all about it in a rambling, in-and-out-of-focus tone.

"You can't imagine what it was like. This witch would be visited in the back of the bakery by the damnedest people—faith healers, spies, stockbrokers, heaven knows what. You'd be amazed at the kinds of people who'll consult a witch if they can find a real one! And this one was real, all right. Sometimes at night her daughter would sneak down-stairs and there in the midst of the good bread-smells and the baking that went on all night, the witch would be talking with—with things from somewhere else, not of this world at all.

"There was one morning when the daughter found the witch-mother emptying out all the ovens. Out of every one

123

came a loaf in the shape of a person, burnt solid black and charred—so horrible, horrible . . .

"And the witch was crying," Mom added, wide-eyed with memory.

I patted her shoulder. "It's all right, Mom," I said, "I can sleep fine now. You don't have to tell any more."

But on she went. "The witch's eyelashes and eyebrows had been scorched right off and it took her months to grow them back again. I wasn't supposed to notice, but I did! The daughter, I mean. Poor kid. She noticed, and she had nightmares afterward. She cried herself to sleep, she was so scared.

"Not that it did any good. The witch-mother went right on with her 'works.' The house rocked with it sometimes. Spells and chants got into the daughter's sleep. It took me years to forget them. Took her years, I mean. The witch even got herself enrolled in some kind of magicians' school called Sorcery Hall. She actually studied the stuff. She loved it.

"But how do you think the daughter felt about all this? You know how a kid wants to be like the other kids? Huh, some chance. Nobody else's mother sat down to tea with semitransparent people or talking houseplants. Do you know what the daughter was most afraid of? That the witch, who was her *mother* after all, would take off for good with her magical friends, leaving behind a fake mother made out of bread."

Poor Mom. She actually shuddered.

I patted her hand. "Did you ever tell Gran how you felt?" I said timidly.

"Who?" she said, blinking at me. "Tell who what?"

"I mean, did the witch's daughter ever tell the witch how she felt about the magic?"

Mom shook her head. "Oh, no, she kept her nightmares to herself. But the witch should have *known*. I mean, what did she think? She was the *mother* and she was a *witch*! Her alma mater wasn't Smith or Brown, it was this Sorcery Hall, where she was studying to become an even witchier witch!" She punched her pillow weakly. "And witches get burned!"

124

I said, "Not Gran. Gran can take care of herself."

"She was just lucky," Mom murmured, subsiding again. Her eyes closed. I suspected that only her memories of outrage were keeping her awake. " 'S not smart to push your luck, even if you've got magic powers. Anything could have happened. She could have died fooling around with magic. She could have . . . vanished. Been carried off somehow, somewhere. Could have . . ."

"But she didn't," I reminded her, thinking of the chance Gran had just taken with the drugged milk. "She wasn't. She won't be."

Mom didn't even hear me. "I didn't want that kind of problem—the daughter didn't, I mean—for her children. She wanted her own daughter to have the luxury of growing up just like the other kids, to lead a normal life. What's wrong with a normal life, anyway? Lots of people have them and like them fine. Any woman just wants a normal life. Even a witch's daughter. 'Specially a witch's daughter. For herself and her own kid."

"Well, you should ask first," I said. "Not every kid is completely sold on 'normal.' "

"You would be," Mom sighed, "if you had the other kind. But you were protected. I protected you, didn't I? Like a good mom. Tried to."

"Yes," I said. "You sure did. Is that the rest of the story?"

"Not the half of it," Mom mumbled. "Witches don't stay married, did you know that? I know it, from experience. That witch didn't keep her husband. The witch's daughter made a bad marriage, too. I mean, a good marriage that fell apart. The man wants to be the powerful one, you know? At least he wants to *think* he is.

"But it's better if he *really* is; if you don't have to pretend . . ."

She smiled, and my scalp crept. I knew she was thinking of Brightner.

I didn't know what to say. I mean, maybe this was the moment, the point at which the right words, the right question or comment could zip right in there and yank my mom back into the real world. Only I didn't know that question or that comment.

"Mom." I floundered. "Mom. Dad didn't take off because of the magic in the family. I don't believe that! And this guy, this other person who's really more powerful"—I almost choked on that part—"he's not the way to go. He's a bad person, Mom. Honestly."

"So the prince came and woke the witch's daughter with a kiss that made her just like all the other girls," Mom said dreamily, "her and her own daughter too, because he was a generous, powerful prince. Nothing witchy about them at all anymore. And they all lived happily—"

"They didn't," I said loudly, right in her face. "They can't! Mom! Don't let him take you away with him, don't!"

"—ever . . . after . . ." Mom tucked her face against her arm to stifle a huge yawn. "There, you've had your story," she mumbled. "Go sleep. Sleep. 'S late."

"I know it's late," I said.

I tickled her hair, which is just this very soft sort of hair-massage from when I was very small and didn't know that hair doesn't feel anything. She used to ask me to do that sometimes, when she was wired from work, to help soothe her down for sleep.

"Is she sleeping?" came the small, scratchy voice of Gran-the-cat.

I jumped a foot. The cat was in the doorway, leaning against the side of it and looking at me with its eyes crossed.

"Yes, I think so," I whispered. How long had Gran been there? Had she heard all that?

"Silly lass," sighed Gran-the-cat, and I thought I heard a break in the voice. She sank down into a sort of oblong puddle of scraggy fur, unsteadily tucking her front paws in under her chest. "I do wish she'd told me. I wish she'd . . . wish I'd . . . wish . . ."

On this last plaintive word, the cat's head dropped forward and hit the floor, nose first, with a soft *thunk*.

126

She stayed just like that, sleeping hard. I could hear from across the room her faint, whistling snores. She looked so helpless and small.

I went and got the handkerchief from my dresser drawer—the handkerchief that had been a flying carpet—and I rolled it up and tied it loosely around the neck of the sleeping cat, wedging the fat part of the rolled cloth so that it made a sort of pillow under the cat's jaw. Even if she slept on the floor, at least she could be comfortable.

Then there was nothing more to do—until the time came to head downtown to Kali's Kitchen, and that was still hours away.

There I was wide awake and jittering with nerves because of what still lay ahead for me to do, while everybody else snoozed around me. If I messed up, they might never wake again.

I got the mirror Barb had given me and studied myself in it. Funny, you wouldn't guess from looking in there that the blond kid with the tired eyes was all whimpery inside from having just too much responsibility on her shoulders. The kid in the glass looked determined.

I put the mirror in my shirt pocket. It would come with me tonight to Kali's Kitchen just, as Barb had said, for luck.

15
Kali's Prize

A trio of diners came wandering out of Kali's Kitchen, yawning and burping and poking around for the armholes of their coats. Lugging the white cotton laundry bag, I ducked past them to enter the restaurant once more. It was well after midnight, edging up on closing time.

Inside, the warm air and red-gold dimness folded around me and my nose began to itch. This was the least of my worries, however. Ushah, draped in a sari of pale blue shot with silver that gleamed as she moved, came rustling out swiftly from behind the register and stood staring at me with smoldering eyes.

In the bag, the doped cat stirred in its sleep so that the bag rotated gently against my leg. If Ushah should notice—

Well, if she noticed, she noticed. I was past fear, or that's the way I felt, anyway. While Ushah looked me over, I took advantage of the pause to note that there were two people still at dinner over by the wall, right under the dancing figure of Kali. Kali's third eye was closed. I found this slightly comforting.

Ushah said softly at last, "My husband said you might come."

"I'm here," I said.

"With your armor on," she sneered, eyeing the silver glove on my left hand.

"He didn't say *not* to wear it," I said cautiously.

"And you bring a package, I see," she added, with a nasty smile. "Why? There is nothing you will be needing."

"He wanted me to bring him some things," I said.

"What things?" She stared at the bag.

"Belongings of my grandmother," I said. "You want to look?"

The two diners were watching us curiously. Ushah, noticing, shrugged the question of the bag away. "This is business of his, not mine. But where is your grandmother? She was to come also. If you have not brought her, these little offerings will not buy you pardon."

"I've talked with my Gran," I said as meekly as I could manage, which was probably not very. "She'll be along a little later."

Ushah smiled again, flashing her mean little pointy teeth at me. "Not too much later, let us hope," she sneered. "My husband is to arrive soon. Meanwhile, you must wait. Take that table there, by the kitchen."

The way she said this, with a contemptuous wave of her hand, made it a deliberate insult. I didn't say a word. I sat down, setting the bag down gently on the floor under the table.

Ushah walked back quickly toward the kitchen, pausing to make some charming comment or other to the two people at the back table and to whisper in passing to the one waiter I saw in the place. He nodded and brought me a glass of water on a tray.

Then he went up front and turned the sign in the

window to read, *Closed*. So soon, so suddenly? It couldn't be closing time, with patrons still in the place! Was Brightner due to walk in at any second?

My table was right next to the little service counter, and under the counter was a big plastic tub of dirty dishes. If there were still dishes to be done, they weren't ready to actually shut down the working part of the restaurant. Better wait, maybe, and not start things yet. Give Gran-the-cat as much rest as I could. Me, too.

But anticipation was rising in me, shooting little lightnings of energy through my body so that I itched to get moving. For one thing, from this angle the image of Kali couldn't see me even if the third eye did open.

The last diners paid their check and left, the Indian Muzak droned along, and the waiter disappeared into the kitchen and didn't come back out through the swinging doors. I heard people calling to each other back there, and the side door banging open against the alley wall and then thumping shut again.

Sooner or later, there would be no one here but Ushah and me. And, at some point, Brightner.

Before he came, Gran and I had to deal with Ushah.

I picked up the laundry bag, carefully laid it out on the table in front of me, and pulled the drawstring loose. The silver glove made the knot fall open in my fingers. With my other hand, I reached inside the bag and touched the round, hard head of the sleeping cat.

"Gran!" I whispered. "Wake up!"

At my back the double doors swished, and Ushah seized the bag with a triumphant shout. Raising it high over her head, she shook out the limp cat onto the carpet at her feet.

"What is this trash you bring here?"

I couldn't draw a breath to answer.

"Ah!" Ushah grinned at me and pounced. Slim fingers closed like iron pincers, and Ushah raised poor Gran triumphantly in the air and shook her by the roll of cloth around her furry neck.

The shaking seemed to blur the form of the cat, elongate it, change it. Ushah herself gave a gasp and dropped the cat.

It landed in the middle of the restaurant floor, suddenly a much larger shape than any cat, and it did something too fast to turn away from and too awful to imagine.

The cat-head jerked inward toward the scrawny chest, like the start of a convulsion, and in the wink of an eye the cat-body turned itself inside out and whipped upright into a new form. I saw a blur of red and white and shining surfaces, a flash of white teeth and bone like the worst scene of a horror movie, all getting bigger and bigger as I watched, my stomach winding up for a good, sick heave.

There stood my Gran, just as I had last seen her, in tweed coat and cowboy boots—with a kerchief tied, bandana-style, around her neck.

I heard a shuddery breath. The waiter was peering out between the swinging doors. I don't know how much he'd seen, but if it was everything I had, then you had to admire his presence of mind.

He said in a high, barely controlled voice, "Good night, good night, Madame, staff are leaving now."

"Go," Ushah barked, without even looking at him.

He sketched a quick sort of salute and ducked back out of sight. With a flurry of whispers and footsteps and the shuddering clang of the alley door, they were gone. We were alone.

A weird hush had fallen in the dining room. I braced myself against the wall where I had stumbled, holding a chair by the uprights of its back. Maybe I was no enchanter myself, but I was ready at that point to try to break the chair over Ushah's head to help Gran.

Ushah moved a few paces sideways, with soundless footfalls like a panther's. She stood under the painting of Kali, her back to it.

I caught my breath with fright.

Kali's third eye peeled itself open. The eye seemed to pulse faintly as I stared at it, like something alive, something

131

hungry. It blazed a hot, evil scarlet with a black center like a hole right into hell.

Ushah, without so much as a glance at Kali, drew herself up as tall as she could and said to Gran in a tone of bitter contempt, "Old woman! You dare to face me?"

My vision seemed as sharp as a razor. I saw the gathered stillness of my grandmother, who was actually an inch or so shorter than Ushah. And I noticed a faint shine of sweat on Ushah's smooth forehead. For all her bold and insulting words, Ushah was *afraid*!

"Ushah," Gran said, and her dry old voice had somehow acquired an echo that seemed to reach away into enormous, invisible distances. "You know me well, as I know you. Listen to me, I have a thing to say to you. Sister, mother, daughter, friend: you have lost your way, you are led astray into danger and disgrace. Take my hand and let me help you back to your path."

She held out her hand, the fingers bent with arthritis. Her expression was not one of anger but of concentration. I saw that Ushah trembled and leaned forward slightly, as if some part of her yearned to respond to Gran's strange offer.

The third eye of Kali began to blaze, and as if in answer so did the caste mark in the middle of Ushah's forehead. Ushah lifted her chin sharply and shouted, "My path is my husband's path—this path!"

She extended her arms and fanned out her fingers in front of her. Beams of black energy seemed to dart from her polished fingernails, reaching for my Gran.

Gran skipped nimbly sideways. A bolt of black energy hit the cash register and melted it into a steaming blob that dripped down off the counter like a watch in a surrealist painting. The air stank of hot metal.

Gran snatched something from the inside of her coat: her reading glasses! I couldn't believe it! What was she going to do, read the riot act to Ushah, who could melt brass? Alzheimer's, I thought wildly; Mom was right, it's true, but what a time for it to hit!

132

I tried to lift the chair off the floor, but I seemed to have no strength in my arms.

"Ushah," Gran said urgently. "That man's way is wicked, false, and cruel. Choose a different way, quickly, while there is yet time!"

For an answer Ushah opened her mouth and screamed something in a voice that rattled the silver on the tables. I had to let go of the chair and cover my ears. I saw Ushah join her hands in front of her, surrounded by flares of dark energy.

"Then, foolish woman," Gran cried fiercely, "follow your chosen path to its end!"

Ushah's black beam sizzled through the air again. Gran thrust out her hand, holding the eyeglasses in front of her like a shield—and the killer beam broke in blinding shards of darkness from one of the tilted lenses.

My head rang with a soundless explosion. I saw the darkness reunite and roll back the way it had come like a huge black wave. The wave dipped down as if bowing to Ushah. It slid under her scrambling feet and surged up again, lifting her on its smoking back. It threw her against the wall behind her.

And the four arms of the painted Kali reached out like spider legs and folded Ushah in.

The struggling witch, her whole face distorted by shrieks that I couldn't hear, simply faded into the painted image. Her flailing arms and legs were fixed, her awful face was just a painting of a fright mask. She went as flat and lifeless as the rest of the picture of Kali dancing and—now—clutching her prize.

A little sign flashed in my mind, "Do Not Feed The Kali," and I giggled wildly. Actually, I felt like throwing up.

Then the paint curled, shriveled, and flaked silently off the wall in a drift of pastel powder. Nothing was left but a pale patch of bare plaster on the wall. The leatherette seats below were lightly coated with fine, multicolored dust.

My legs gave out and I sat down with a gasp on the carpeted floor.

"Wow," I said, hearing my own voice like something under water. But at least I heard it.

"Wow with knobs on," Gran said a little shakily. She put down on the nearest table the twisted ruins of her reading glasses. "I wasn't really up for that, not right off the bat."

"You got her," I said. "You got her, Gran!" I would have danced, if I could have made my legs hold me.

"She got herself," Gran said bitterly. "A fine young power in the world has been perverted till it had to be destroyed."

"But how—?" I remembered what she had said to me about strafing Brightner from the flying carpet. "You turned her strength back on her," I said. "You reflected it back with your glasses."

"I did indeed," she said. "I sent back what she sent me."

"Wait till I tell Barb," I babbled. "I've seen it with my own eyes, it's just like she says: what goes around, comes around!"

Gran said in a quiet, thoughtful voice, "Oh, yes, lovie, it does. That puts it very well." She stretched. "Good, I'm feeling better. There's nothing like being forced to your uttermost to get the blood stirring again, is there? I feel almost ready for him!"

"What's that?" I said. Now that my hearing was back, I seemed to hear more sharply than before. And what I heard was a faint jangling noise from the back of the restaurant, and then a hollow boom that was alarmingly familiar. "That's the alley door banging against the wall outside!"

"Hurry!" Gran said.

I followed her through the swinging doors and the kitchen, and there was the alley door gaping wide, and out in the alley itself—

"Stay back," Gran said, catching my wrist.

I did, but I leaned out and looked.

134

I saw Ushah's bicycle, The Great Galloping Claw, speeding toward the street. Scattering before it were half a dozen shadows like thin black gauze whipped along in a stiff wind.

As we watched, the bike turned onto the street and wheeled out of sight.

"The basement," I said. "Maybe there are some left!"

But Gran's crooked fingers tightened on my wrist. "Don't waste your time," she said. "The Claw will have rounded them all up for him, never fear, and we must hurry! I should have realized that he'd have a spy-hole here—the eye of Kali, like as not! He won't come against me here, not now, with victory fresh in my hands. It's too chancy. He'll want an edge, lovie, like any bully!"

She hurried me out of the restaurant door.

"But where are we going?" I said, catching something from her—excitement, even eagerness.

"Where he'll be waiting," she said, "hoping to snare the pair of us—at Wollman rink, the root of your mother's dream. That's where he'll have done it—used her power to make a great vortex, a magical engine to launch himself and all his booty straight for the wizard war!"

16

On Brightner's Ice

There was always the chance, of course, that Brightner would get impatient and take off with what he already had, never mind Gran and me. Impatient, or nervous.

After what had happened to Ushah, the possibility of him chickening out rather than squaring off with my Gran didn't seem so crazy. My mood swung wildly between terror that we would get to Wollman and find that he'd gone, and a sniveling, craven hope that that was how it *would* be—so that we wouldn't have to face him, fight him, win back my mother and the harvest of captive souls, which I saw now as one giant task: the task of beating Brightner.

Not that Gran and I could discuss this openly in the cab on our way to the park, which was a kind of a relief to me, actually. I wasn't proud of my own attacks of cowardice.

The cabbie thought we were crazy, anyway. All the way up Sixth Avenue, he gave us an argument about driving into the park at that hour, let alone letting us off in the middle of it. He steered with one hand and turned to squint back at the two of us as if we were Martians.

"I don't get it," he said. "I thought even out-of-towners knew better. You're talking about *Central Park*, lady. Which is full of muggers and worse."

"Muggers," Gran said, "are by and large lazy, self-indulgent folk. They will have all made their hauls by now or given up because of the night chill. Hurry, please."

"Hurry, she says," he said, shaking his head wonderingly. "You know those hansom cabs that take tourists for rides in there at night? Why do you think they clop along in caravans, one after the other like a goddamn camel train, eh? Why do they do that? Because of the muggers, that's why."

"Yes or no?" Gran said crisply.

The cabbie scowled. "It'd be murder to let the two of you off alone in the middle of the park at this hour!"

He was already slowing down to stop outside the park wall when I had my inspiration. "We won't be alone," I said. "We're meeting someone."

"Who, King Kong?" the driver said.

"As a matter of fact he's an ex-cop and he's over six feet tall and weighs maybe two hundred pounds. He's lethal. *Nobody* messes with him," I said. (Except us, of course. The cabbie was right: we were crazy.)

He sighed. "Okay, all right. I'll take you in."

He swung the cab in at the entrance where Sixth Avenue dead-ends on the southern border of the park. The dark gap in the black stone boundary wall swallowed us up, and we tore along past the outposts of yellow light from the cast-iron lampposts strung out along cement paths winding into the blackness of trees and bushes.

I sat nervously smoothing the soft leather of the glove over my left hand.

We stopped, at Gran's instructions, where the drive passes between the carousel building, invisible at night in its little tree-shaded hollow, and the chess-and-checkers hill.

No sign of Brightner; was he here? My heart hammered and my eyes felt as if they would pop out of my head, I was staring so hard into the shadows.

Gran fished a bill out of her coat pocket.

"So where is he, this giant ex-cop you're meeting?" the driver said, looking at the money.

"Up there," I said, pointing up the steps to the chess pavilion. "With his telescope."

"Stargazing," the cabbie sighed, "at three in the morning in the middle of Central Park! Now I've seen everything." He took the bill and gave it a squinty look: probably thought we were trying to palm off some Martian money on him. You could tell he wouldn't put anything past us—people who wanted to be dropped in the park at night!

"Keep the change," Gran said.

He shook his head again and drove away fast.

I couldn't help wondering if I would live to ride in a New York taxi again.

The pitch-blackness between the lights was thick with quiet, and in the quiet came sounds so small and quick that you couldn't even guess what had made them. The shadows around us seemed to shift and stir, even though there wasn't a single breath of wind. It was one of those nights when the lights of the nighttime city were diffused and reflected back from a low flat layer of clouds, throwing a murky pallor over everything. The air smelled of damp earth and dead leaves, and the actual sky was completely hidden.

I felt as if my ears were standing out a foot from my head on either side, I was listening so hard for a whisper, a sound of footsteps besides our own.

"Up the hill, hurry," Gran said.

At the top of the chess-and-checkers hill, all we found was just what's supposed to be up there: a brick pavilion with eight sides sitting in the middle of a paved terrace of concrete game-tables and benches. The pavilion was locked up tight (I could make out some chairs and tables inside, behind the grimy windows). The weathercock on the roof stood in silent silhouette against the glowing clouds.

The south side of the hill overlooks the sunken site of the Wollman Memorial Skating Rink.

We stood at an angle of the railing of metal pipe that skirts the terrace, looking over a shoulder of rough black granite sticking out of the hilltop. Trees reached up at us from the shadowed slope below. Farther down came the darkness of the little valley, and enclosed by a fence in the middle of that darkness—Wollman, thrown into sharp relief by floodlights mounted high on metal poles.

I shivered and shivered, though there was no wind. I turned up the collar of my jacket and stuffed my hands deep into my pockets, and I still shivered.

It seemed to me that I was looking down at a dead, ugly animal lying in its cage of chain-link fencing. The animal was the building, a deserted hulk. All its colorless lifeblood had oozed into a flat, solidified plate—the featureless concrete pad spread out behind it. A big yellow crane, with its arm sticking up into the sky like the antennae of a giant insect, stood to one side like the winner of one of those tremendous battles of monsters in Japanese horror flicks: *Wollzilla Meets Cranera*.

Gran said, "This is the place of your mother's dream, the dream she's trapped in."

"But where is she?" I said, whispering in spite of myself. "And where's the phantom rink that I saw at Rockefeller Plaza? And the thing, what did you call it? The vortex?"

"They are one and the same," Gran said grimly, "and it's all here, with its master. He's hiding in shadow, waiting for me to make the first move. Well, so I shall. Do you know chess?" She turned and tapped the top of the nearest chess table with her crooked fingers.

"Um, no," I said. "I know some card games."

Gran shook her head. "What other games do you play with your friends?"

139

"Monopoly," I said. "Battleship." I have seldom felt myself to be such a totally inadequate baby as at that moment.

"All right, we'll use a computer model instead." Gran began sort of typing on the squares of the chessboard, the way you type on a computer keyboard.

Instantly, the entire cloud-cover vanished. We stood under a clean arch of night, with the few stars that can be seen over a big city. The moon was large and bright.

But there was still no Brightner, no phantom rink.

"*Bloody* hell," Gran swore. "He's resisting, trying to wear me down right at the beginning! And I'm already tired, lovie, more tired than I thought. I was mad to waste my strength struggling with Ushah. Oh, I'm an old show-off, I'm an old fool!"

"Gran," I said, "stop blaming yourself and fight!"

"Because I knew her," Gran groaned, "I took the time to try to win her back. Heavens, the arrogance—I should have just flattened the creature straightaway—"

"Gran!" I pulled her arm hard. "Please!"

She turned away from me and didn't answer.

In that moment the heart sort of fell out of me. I thought I would die where I stood—of helplessness and of defeat, I guess. Gran's and mine.

"Coward!" I screamed down at the little valley. "Come out and fight!"

I heard laughter, spattering on the terrace around us like fat drops of rain.

He shouldn't have laughed. Gran turned slowly and faced me again. "I only have so much left in me," she said slowly, "but it might do. If you'll be the bait, lovie. Will you?"

"Sure! What do I do?" I said. Bait! This didn't sound so great, but anything was better than giving up.

Gran sat down on one of the benches. "Help me off with these boots," she said.

I knelt and tugged them off her tiny, lumpy feet.

She nodded. "Now, you put them on."

140

I looked at the boots. They were too big for her—she wore two pairs of thick socks underneath—but still way too small for me. I said so.

"Put them on, lovie," Gran said. "They'll fit."

They did. But when I stood up, I staggered: the boots had blades under them. They weren't scraped and battered cowboy boots anymore, but scraped and battered white figure skates. I stared down at them.

"Going skating?" Brightner's voice said out of the sky in a husky, smiling tone. "Come on down. The ice is nice and fresh."

"Weaver of lies!" Gran shouted suddenly. "Then show it!"

Down below, like a ghostly overlay across the stillness of the closed-down rink, I saw movement: darkness turning, a crowd of figures that were shadows still but each lit faintly from inside by imprisoned light. Brightner's captured souls skated in the phantom rink where Wollman should have been.

And at the center of their slow, gloomy wheeling, Brightner, his fists akimbo, looked up at us. Behind him I saw flashes of my mother's blue ski jacket, of her auburn hair. He hid her from us with his own bulk, except these glimpses as he took small, curving steps from side to side on his skates. Taunting, teasing.

His voice rang through the air: "How do you like it? Hey, old woman? Can you do as much?"

"I can do better!" Gran flung back, grabbing my arm and pulling herself to her feet. I tottered in the skates, but kept my balance. "Any wholesome living spirit could do better than a follower of the left-hand path, the path of fear and force and lies!"

"You told the kid you could beat me," he shouted. "Isn't that a lie?"

"I told her we would try," Gran retorted. "And that's true!"

"Come down and let's talk about it," he answered. "The

141

kid can use the skates. You don't need them. There are plenty of branches up there—make yourself a broom and fly down!"

"I'll fly a flag, not a broom," Gran shouted, and her hand tightened on my arm. "A banner! A bridge! Look!"

She untied the kerchief from her neck and shook it out, a rectangle of cloth—the handkerchief that had been our flying carpet, its pattern all black and gray and white in the moonlight. From her upflung hand it unrolled in a changed shape, long and narrow, light enough to float on the air. It had become a silky scarf.

Gran held the scarf high by both corners and snapped it above her head. The pattern vanished as if her motion had flicked it off. The shining white cloth soared, light as a leaf on the wind, arching away from us and down over the edge of the hill, holding its curved and graceful shape in the empty air. It made a pale, thin path that swooped down past the dark rock and the tree branches—all the way to the edge of the phantom rink far below.

Holding her end of the scarf delicately in both hands, Gran said to me from between clenched teeth, "He's waiting, and it's all I can do to tend your path for you, lovie. You must do the rest."

I couldn't see Brightner anymore. The swirling crowd of silent skaters had thickened and darkened, hiding him.

"But I don't know what to do," I protested weakly. What *could* I do, standing there chilled through and shaking? How could I save my mom and the poor doomed phantoms? How could I stop Brightner, the necromancer, the slaver, the rogue?

"You must skate this path to Brightner's ice," Gran said, "and bring your mother back. He's made her the keystone of this theft of souls, and we must hope that without her, it will all collapse around him. All—the theft of souls, the theft of your mother and her unused power! Otherwise—he'll take you, lovie, and reel me in at the end of this bit of magic of

142

mine. It's not just your mother but you and me too that will go trailing off in Brightner's chains!"

"Bring Mom back how?" I quavered.

"Not my way," Gran said. "Your way, which you must find for yourself. To start, step forward."

She bent and held the scarf-end low off the pavement, and somehow or other, fighting the resistance of my terrified body, I put one foot on the gossamer surface, thinking shakily, if it's too hard, I can always change my mind.

The skates whipped me away down the silken path with my arms flailing and a scream trailing behind me.

I flew out beyond the hilltop, crouching over blades that carried me with soundless speed on the scarf-path—an icily glittering ribbon arched through thin air. Then down went the path and down I went, swooping at an impossible angle into the valley under the hill and up again, sickeningly, toward the jagged top of the chain-link fence, toward the phantom skaters massed beyond it.

I couldn't see my mom, but I knew where she was: at the center.

With him.

The wind of my speed tore water from the corners of my eyes as I flew toward the wheel of shadows. I could have turned aside, I think; sheer speed would have carried me somewhere, anywhere, besides onto Brightner's ice.

But I no longer wanted to turn. I held my breath, lowered my head, and hit the wall of shadows like a human battering ram.

And shot right through. They flowed over my back like streamers. Their voices sighed in my ears. I felt faint, cold pluckings and tuggings at my hair and my sleeves. Shreds of darkness caught and clung to me, plastered to my face like black scarves. With my gloved hand, I tore at the silky layers that bound my eyes like the webs of giant spiders.

The darkness peeled away, and on my hand the glove blazed with a silver light as blinding as a star. I tucked my gloved hand behind me, but my eyes were still dazzled.

Terrified of rushing headlong to a crash, I flung my bare right hand out in front of me.

It was grabbed. I was checked and swung in a dizzying circle to a hard, stumbling stop.

"What about that!" Brightner said in that smug, plummy voice. "She told me you'd come along like a good girl. And here you are. Well, don't just stand there—you're not cannon fodder, like the others. You travel first class, with your mother. Step into the magic circle, we have to go."

I tried to pull away from him, but I was stuck—my left hand was caught, too. Heart pounding, I looked back.

The brilliance of the glove was completely quenched, hidden by a thick wad of hot, heavy shadow stuff that stuck to my whole forearm like a blob of black cotton candy spun out of lead.

Brightner's hold on my right hand was very light but it might as well have been a grip of steel. I sort of hung there off the tips of his fingers, just outside the ring of orange cones that marked off the center of the ice. I was trapped, pulled taut between him and his shadow-caught, captive souls.

He wore his gray suit and black skating boots with thin blue lines like lightning running up the sides. I looked up at his moist-lipped, twinkle-eyed smile. He was so big and solid and packed with a kind of darkly shining strength that I quaked. How had we ever thought to challenge him, Gran and me?

My ankles felt like caving in; my left hand was dragged down by dark, heavy weight while my right lay cool and resistless in his. My shoulders were killing me.

"That hurts," I said, and it came out a sob.

"Not here in the magic circle," he said. "I can heal pain, here. What's holding you back?" he mocked. "You should have listened to me and taken off that grimy old glove."

"I want my mom," I whimpered.

"Here she is, inside the magic circle," Brightner said lightly. "Waiting for you."

144

Behind him at the exact center of the circle, my mom turned slowly, eyes closed, arms lifted and floating like a bird's wings.

"Mom!" I wailed.

She didn't even open her eyes.

I twisted to look back up at the chess-and-checkers hill. My glittering path shot up into nothingness. A vast darkness shut me in on every side. With Brightner.

"Gran, help!" I cried.

"But she's with me," he said. "Your Gran. Here in the magic circle. She gave in before you did. She tricked you into my hands as part of the price for the endless life I can give her. Don't you see her?"

I did. I saw Gran in her tweed coat and cowboy boots, standing on the ice with her face turned away from me.

"Gran," I choked.

No. She was wearing cowboy boots—the boots that had changed into the skates I was wearing on my feet! That wasn't Gran. It was one of Brightner's lies.

"Come along," he said. "We can't wait forever. There are battles to be fought! Step forward. Just say, 'I will,' and my new recruits will release your other hand. You'll see how good they are already at obeying orders."

How else could I get to Mom? And that I had to do, at any price, even if—even if it meant being kidnapped by Brightner himself. I just couldn't let Mom be whisked away, helpless and enchanted, to some strange and horrible place all alone. My mom who was *afraid* of magic, who didn't have a clue about how to use her own abilities, who couldn't even begin to defend herself!

"I will," I whispered. My left hand came suddenly free. I stumbled between the orange cones into the magic circle, hugging my burning hand to my chest.

The glove was gone. My fingers were bare, red, and stinging, curled together without any strength in them at all. I tried to pull my right hand away from Brightner, but it was as if I had wedged it into a crack in a boulder.

145

"How would you like to make the journey?" he said in the smooth, juicy tone of somebody savoring some particularly delicious flavor. "Now that you've given up the pathetic 'protection' of the glove to my troops, there, everything becomes possible. Want to go in the form of a bad-mannered little cat shut up in a laundry bag? Or maybe as a fat, ragged bag lady, reduced to the size of a silver charm to hang on my watch chain?"

I was too scared to even wonder if he could really do those things to me. The bones in my right hand and arm felt as if they were melting and bending in his grip.

He twisted my hand and I slid to one side, squalling with pain. He turned gracefully on his skates, smiling into my face, twisting and crushing. I could no more resist than I could get an A in math. My feet, scrabbling for purchase on the ice, flew out in opposite directions. I was going to hit the ice hard because he wanted me to hit the ice hard, and he was strong enough to make it happen the way he wanted it to.

Turn his strength against him.

On a reckless, raging impulse, I threw myself into the fall like a suicide leaping off a cliff. The back of my shoulders slammed into Brightner's legs, which shot out from under him. I slid on my belly like a collapsed starfish—free. I felt the tremor in the ice when he landed, and I gasped with joy.

I knew I'd done something, though I didn't dare to think what. I looked around, my eyes stretched wide like a scared animal's.

I saw Brightner, yards away, sit up slowly, holding the back of his head. The false image of Gran was gone. All around us Brightner's souls came pouring silently in toward the center of the ice, knocking the orange cones every which way. The only sound was the dry skittering of the cones on the ice.

I scrambled up and staggered toward my mom. I threw my arms around her—around nothing that I could hold.

146

I was stunned. He hadn't fetched my mom yet—this was only the reflection of her, not even as she really was, scrubbed and sleeping at home, but as she had been when she went skating with Brightner—dressed for the outdoors and made up to slay.

Could I reverse the magic—fetch the "fetch" back to the real woman? How would you take a reflection from one place to another?

With shaking hands I fumbled out of my shirt pocket the little makeup mirror Barb had given me. I wobbled backward on my skates, holding up the little oval of glass. "Look!" I sobbed. "Mom, you have to see how you look—for *him!*"

That did it. The dreaming eyes opened and looked: at the glass, and then, bewildered, at me.

In the space of about a second and a half, the fetch faded and was gone—into the glass, where a reflection belonged? I didn't dare look to see, for fear of canceling her reflection by laying my own over it. But my heart pounded with hope. He had saved the fetching of my mom till last, till Gran and I could be captured, too—maybe because once the vital power at the heart of his whole scheme—my mom—actually stepped as her real self into his vortex-engine here at Wollman, that engine would take off, no longer in his complete control. He was greedy, just as Gran said—he wanted us, too, in the vortex. So he had waited. And we had a chance.

I stuffed the mirror back into my shirt and got out of there—or tried to. The skates no longer carried me effortlessly along. I had to drive them with my bruised and wobbly legs, and keep my balance, too.

The shadows, their inner gleams of light much brighter now so that "shadow" was not the word for them anymore, drew apart before me and closed after me. There was a silvery shine to them, as if they had absorbed the glow of the glove they had taken from me, and suddenly I had no fear of them at all. I thought I felt them urging me on, toward the

147

stark white path which rose at the edge of the ice only twenty yards away.

Behind me Brightner roared, "Laura, come back! Tina! Damn you, kid, you get back here to me *now!*"

A frantic glance over my shoulder showed me only the silver skaters: hiding me, shielding me! Could that be?

Something enormous crashed down near me, sending great black cracks jagging through the ice, and whipped away through the air again leaving me staggered as if by the jetstream of a passing semi. Stunned and dismayed—what now, with escape so close?—I looked up.

The huge iron hook at the end of the crane cable hurtled through the air and smashed down again, a foot from me.

Beyond the edge of the ice, the squat yellow cab of the crane strained backward off its tanklike treads, tilting its long black latticework arm. The hook was jerked out of the ice with a dry, groaning sound, and it swung back through the dark in a ponderous arc. Then cab and arm dropped heavily forward again, and the cable lashed from the end of the arm across the sky. The hook hurtled toward me like a bomb.

The Claw.

I threw myself aside and hugged the ice. Everything shook. Flying ice chips stung my cheek.

I scrambled up and skated like crazy for the path. Brightner's ice was disintegrating under me, broken by a spreading web of inky cracks. Rough and soft, the ice gave under my blades so that I could hardly make headway.

Another jolting crash of the iron hook, and the whole ice-surface began to sink, but I was at the path—

There was no more path. Instead, the end of Gran's long scarf dangled in the air in front of me, above the moving ice.

I made a wild leap and grabbed, clinging frantically as the scarf lifted me into the night as if it were being reeled up on a giant spool in the sky. I twisted my legs and feet into the fabric the way you do when you climb ropes in the gym at school. But this stuff was slicker than those rough old

148

ropes, and my hands weren't working too well in the holding-on department.

If I fell—well, it was a long way down, now, to Brightner's ice.

The iron hook lanced upward, whooshing through the sky after me to the full stretch of the crane cable.

The glinting mass sliced past the blades of my skates, and then it went down, and down, pulled by its own momentum. It slammed into the center of Brightner's ice and shattered it into a slow fountain of big white slabs that leaped like angular dolphins. From the center of the plunging ice burst Brightner's souls, captive no longer. They streamed past me into the night sky, brightening in the moonlight like a meteor shower as they arced down again, drifted briefly over the city, and vanished.

He had lost them, and all over the city their abandoned bodies would be coming to life again as the freed souls settled back into them.

Below, the yellow crane, dragged forward by its own cable, sank down into the darkness that the chunks of ice seemed to float on. It all began to spin, oily blackness and bobbing ice, in a slow spiral around the place where the hook had gone in and pulled the crane down after it.

Brightner, alone now on the largest slab of ice, skated furiously in a tight circle.

Breathless, hanging onto my scarf-in-the-sky like a monkey on a rope, I stared down at him. *You lose*, I thought fiercely; *you lose!*

He hadn't given up, though. He was trying to build enough momentum to leap to another chunk of ice further away, and another, until he could reach the solid ground of the plain nighttime park and escape.

There! He sprang like a tiger—but the ice upended and sank under his foot as he took off. I saw him turn in the air, his arms upflung and his mouth open in a wild howl, and the inky blaze of his eyes stabbed at me. Then he dropped like a black stone into the center of the vortex, and the roaring, spinning wall of ice and darkness closed on him and sank, drilling down into the heart of the world, where it vanished.

Nothing was left behind but the flat pale slab of the real Wollman rink, harmless and still.

I laughed; at least, I think that's what I was doing. These high, silly sounds kept shaking out of me, and then the sky-scarf cracked itself like a whip, flicking me off. My mouth was full of the wind of falling.

I landed with a jolt that knocked a yelp out of me. There was cold stone under my forearms and stone under my butt. Across the small table from me sat two people, clearly visible in the glow of the rising sun: my Gran, her face pillowed on her folded arms, snoring gently; and my mom, who squinted at me and said plaintively, "Valli, what on earth am I doing out here at sunrise in my bathrobe and these awful carpet slippers?"

On the checkered tabletop between us were bits of glass, shards of the mirror that must have been jarred out of my pocket when I landed. The scattered slivers reflected the bright, clean light of a dawn I had been sure I would never see.

17

Slime-coated Men

Crows cawed, a traffic helicopter rattled by overhead. Day, I thought. Imagine that. Morning in Central Park. And the fetch, let loose from the mirror, had gone and fetched my mom—to me.

I said, "Hi, Mom."

"Hi, yourself," she said, squinting blearily at me. She stood up, not very steadily. "Come on, let's go home. We'll talk about this later."

But you know, we never did. Not really.

Afterward, when I heard her telling people that she'd had to go away for a few days to identify an old lady who might be my missing Gran, I didn't say anything. And when Mom told close friends that Gran had lived as a homeless person, in shelters and churches and so on, for a few days until I had somehow tracked her down in the park, well, I let that go by, too.

I had about three days out of school—which I spent in

bed, resting—while my hands healed. Not that you could see anything wrong with them, but I couldn't hold a pencil or a pen for a while. They got better gradually, and steadily enough so that the doctor didn't mind so much not having a clue to what was wrong with them in the first place.

Then I discovered that while I had always been definitely right-handed, I was now totally ambidextrous, which was fun (amaze your friends) but confusing, until I began to get used to it.

One night while I was still in bed Gran brought me some take-out food for dinner.

Not Chinese. Indian.

"What's wrong?" she said. "There's nothing inherently sinister about Indian food, you know."

I shrank back from the steaming cartons on the tray. "I'm allergic," I said, remembering a certain betraying sneeze.

"Nonsense, lovie," Gran said. "You're not sensitive to black spices but to the black magic that was mixed in with them. Try some of this."

She insisted that I eat some kind of pureed eggplant dish, which looked like mud and tasted wonderful. "Gran," I said around a luscious mouthful, "how come Kali worked for Brightner?"

"He chose an ancient image of evil and infused it with his own will," Gran said. "As I might have allied my strengths to an Indian concept of good, Krishna, for example, and used that. Ushah gave Brightner easy access to the worst elements of her native religion, which was one reason she was useful to him. Poor Ushah."

"Phooey," I said, without a whole lot of conviction though, I will never forget the sight of Ushah caught in the arms of the painted Kali.

We ate and watched TV for a while. (The pickled onions were also terrific.)

We had had a number of meals together like this since that night in the park, with Gran perched on my bed eating from the other side of the tray. Gran was staying with us

152

while looking, with Mom, for another retirement place to move into.

This made things crowded for a while (especially in the mornings when everybody needed the bathroom at once), but wonderful. Gran and I had a lot to talk over.

This particular night, the night of the Indian take-out dinner, Gran said that the captured souls had been able to escape the collapse of the ice because of strength they had drawn from the silver glove, which they had more or less eaten off my hand. Talk about magic food!

"What a beautiful meteor shower that was," Gran said, "when everyone who had been under Brightner's power broke free! A good night's work, lovie."

This kind of talk made me uncomfortable, I guess because I didn't see myself as some kind of hero. I mean, that's something out of a book or a movie, not a person's life. I was still Valentine Marsh, and I had to go back to school in a few days. So I tried to stay casual about this other stuff.

"All that, with one little glove?" I said. "I should go look around for the matching one!"

"Oh, you have it," Gran said. "That sort of magic is never used up, you know, only changed. Brightner underestimated its power, or he would never have let his phantoms near the glove. Imagine thinking they would destroy it! All they wanted was to draw strength from it so they could pull free of him. They knew what it was: a form of love. Which is what all good magic boils down to, anyway, just as all bad magic boils down to fear, and force, and lies."

I chewed, thinking about this and what it naturally brought to mind. "What about The Claw?" I said. I still dreamed about that thing.

"His own malice, embodied," Gran said. "And it pulled him down in the end."

While we sat thinking solemn thoughts about this (mine were mostly along the lines of "Good, good, good!"), Mom came in, carrying packages.

She glanced at the open food cartons and sniffed the air.

"Indian food?" she said. "I hate the stuff. Good thing there's some leftover chicken, unless somebody ate it for lunch today."

She had been leaving us alone together a lot, almost as if she wanted to give us room to talk about things that she didn't want any part of, herself. This time was different. We had our only conversation together about what had happened with Dr. Brightner, and it went more or less as follows.

"I want you to know," Mom said, appearing in the doorway with a half-stripped chicken carcass, "both of you, that I'm very grateful. I also feel like an idiot." Nobody objected to this. Mom went on, "I'm not even really sure of what happened—" She held up fingers shiny with chicken to stop us from telling her.

"And I don't want to know, all right? I don't want to know any more than I think I remember, which is hair-raising and embarrassing enough."

Gran sighed. "Good heavens, Laura, didn't you learn anything? All this only happened because you've refused to learn about things that are crucial to our family—"

"That's right," Mom interrupted. "I refused, and I still refuse. But I do want to know what it means for Val, having had this kind of—experience. It's not the first time, as we all know. Is it, finally, going to be the last?"

She looked at me so anxiously that I squirmed.

Gran scooped up mango chutney in a pocket of fried bread. "That depends on Val," she said. "It's all a matter of choice, Laura."

"Val?" Mom said.

I shrugged and looked at my plate. "I don't know, Mom. I guess if magic runs in the family, I'll have to decide. Not yet, though. I think I'm burned out, for the time being."

"For the time being." Mom aimed the chicken accusingly at Gran. "You're encouraging her! I told you after the last time, when it was statues and sea-monsters and God knows what. I thought you understood me, I thought we had agreed that that was *it*. And now this—! Once and for all, I don't want Val involved in any more weirdness!"

"She is involved," Gran said patiently. "Because of who she is."

"Oh, who she is!" Mom said. "In my opinion, Val hasn't been herself for some time now. Did you know that she's been taking money from my purse for months?"

Well, my face felt like flames.

Gran looked at me. "Val, I'm surprised at you."

I tried to say something but nothing came. I am talking terminal embarrassment here.

Gran said, "I'm sure it's just a phase, Laura. It won't go on, particularly now that you've brought the matter out into the open. And I never said the child is perfect, only that she is gifted."

"I don't want her to be 'gifted,'" Mom protested. "Not that way!"

"Mom," I said, "come on. If I didn't have *something*, I couldn't have, well, helped Gran make things come out all right that night at Wollman." I could see by Mom's expression that if I went on about that, I'd lose her. So I shifted course. "Anyway, it's not as if I'm packing tonight to go study at Sorcery Hall. I won't even consider anything like that yet."

At the mention of Sorcery Hall, Mom's face sort of crumpled as if she was holding back tears. "This isn't some silly game, it's dangerous! And you two do nothing but back each other up against me!" she cried, and she turned hurriedly and went to her bedroom.

Gran and I looked at each other.

"I tried," I said.

"You did fine," Gran said gently. "It's not so easy when you know that, much as you love your mother, and much as she loves you, you're braver than she is."

That stuff again! Could it be that Gran didn't know how scared I was most of the time we were fighting Brightner?

Anyway, if there's one thing I've learned, it's that nobody can be brave all the time, certainly not me. And Mom can't be a weakling and still do her job for her authors and keep going in publishing, which is a business that looks like it's dying out half the time.

On the other hand, Gran was generally right, so I wasn't going to argue. Besides, I had something else on my mind.

"Listen," I said, "you know what she said that night, about how she hated you being a witch? And you said you wished you'd known. If you had known how she felt while she was a little kid, would you have quit?"

Gran carefully dabbed at the corners of her mouth— which had a tendency to leak slightly when she was eating— with a neatly folded paper napkin. She gazed at the TV screen for a second.

Then she said, "No. The gift was mine, and I chose to use it. But I might have found ways to try to make it all easier on poor Laura. Why do you ask? Are you thinking about resigning your own capacities to ease your mother's mind?"

I considered this while Gran demolished another puff of thin, fried bread stuffed with chutney.

I said, "What if I do resign?"

"That's up to you," she said. "But I can tell you, lovie, that deciding, for someone else's sake, not to use your own strength is usually a poor choice, with sad lessons in it and precious little joy."

I ate more pickled onions. "Actually, I think I'll stick with the family gift," I said.

Gran licked crumbs off her lips—for a second there she reminded me of a certain little gray alley cat—and said, "That decision will have its own costs, you realize. There are lessons in every choice you make, and not all lessons can be fun."

I sighed. No sugarcoated reassurances from Gran. "I can hack it," I said.

I hope I can.

To tell the truth, I am not sorry that Mom wants no part

of magic for herself. Even without special powers, she knows things you wouldn't expect her to. Any more of that and life could be pretty uncomfortable.

Speaking of which, she has never mentioned my pilfering again, maybe because I've quit doing it. It just doesn't seem to fit me anymore.

Not that I'm some different person than I was, deep down, and my friends recognize me all right. Barb came to visit while I was still in bed.

"So how'd things turn out?" she said, as soon as we were alone.

I told her.

She sat and thought for about five minutes. Then she said, "Listen, Valentine. Next time something like this comes up, I want to know about it right away. If you ever go off on some kind of magical adventure without me again, I will never forgive you."

"Sure," I said. "I'm sorry about the mirror."

"Don't be sorry," she said. "It did you some good, right? That's what it was for." She grinned delightedly. "I don't believe it! That dinky little mirror *helped*!"

"It sure did," I said fervently. "Listen, you can have anything I've got, Barb, just name it, okay?"

She reared back and looked at me from under lowered lids. "Did I say I was selling you my mirror? Did I say I was trading it for something? Wouldn't mind borrowing your Auntie Jailbreak records for my next party, though."

"It's a deal," I said. "How'd it go with, you know, your own problem?"

Barb made a face. "Brother picked up his stuff and left home, he just walked out, after all that fuss. And he took my Walkman with him. He is on his own from now on, believe me. Barbara is going to be too busy on her own life to get messed around on account of him, wherever he is."

Well, maybe. I know a thing or two more about family loyalty than I did before.

Barb was a great audience. Talking to her kind of loosened up some of the tension the whole business had left thrumming around in my nerves. She made me tell it all to her about six times, till I said I was all talked out.

Then she grinned and said, "Got something for you. I don't think it's magic, but it will make you laugh." She got a newspaper clipping out of her bookbag and gave it to me. "From Lennie," she said. "He asked me to give it to you."

"SLIME-COATED MEN ARRESTED NEAR MILLIONS," the headline said. I read the item out loud, with proper dramatic emphasis. No, it wasn't about giant snail-men from Pluto captured at a football game. It was about some Italian burglars who got caught trying to break into the central post office in Rome to steal a payroll—by sneaking in through the sewers.

Mom stuck her head into my room, her glasses shoved up on her forehead. She did most of her work from home that week, especially during the part when I couldn't use my hands too well. "It's not enough to pass notes in class, now you're doing it at home? What for—practice? What's so funny, anyway?"

I showed her the clipping. "Good grief," she chortled. "Where did you find this?"

"Lennie sent it," I said. "His father gets lots of newspapers. When I go over there after school, sometimes we look through the stack for the most outrageous headlines we can find."

Mom handed it back.

"Well, keep it down to a dull roar in here, will you?" she said. "I've got a contract to discuss with one of my authors, and it takes away from my agently dignity if he hears screams of girlish laughter in the background."

I told Barb, "Tell Lennie this one is a real winner. Tell him I'm glad to hear from him."

"Sure," she said. "Now tell me again how your Gran fed Ushah to Kali-on-the-wall."

When I got back to school with a note from my old therapist about how I hadn't really been cutting school, only looking for my Gran, I went to the office of the school psychologist. Imagine my surprise: there was Miss Matthews. Word had it that somehow her marriage had turned out to be illegal or something. Or maybe it just didn't turn out. Anyway, here she was back, all perky and chin-up and pretending she had never been shunted aside by circumstances to make room for the dreaded Dr. Brightner to move in on me in my own school.

I did actually mention this to her.

"I understand that this Dr. Brightner was a pretty impressive guy," she said, "but apparently unstable, to have just vanished the way he did. Never let it be said that we psychologists are immune to mental troubles of our own."

"Never," I agreed, "especially the ones who aren't really psychologists at all. Like Brightner."

"Now, Valentine," she said firmly, "just because you didn't like the man, that's no reason to make wild accusations now that he's not around to defend himself."

"You wouldn't like it much if he were," I began, pushed by an impulse to spill it all and blow her mind. But the look she gave me made it clear that much more of that and I'd be seeing her regularly, so I left it alone.

Lennie, having made his peace offering with Slime-coated Men, has heard part of the story and is still chewing that over. He says a little at a time is fine with him. He's trying to get used to the idea of me having a magical grandmother, never mind my being responsible for upheavals at school and the rescue of my own mom from an evil wizard.

"Valentine Marsh," he says sometimes, slowly and thoughtfully. He looks at me and shakes his head. "Valentine Marsh. You are really something."

I did actually manage to catch up on my homework by nearly killing myself. School is important. I'm thinking about eventually applying to Duke or some other place where they do research on the so-called paranormal.

I've spotted Dirty Rose once or twice, making her garbage-can rounds. The one time I tried to get close enough to give her a candy bar I had in my pocket, she scurried away muttering wildly over her shoulder at me. Whatever ironing

159

out of the mental kinks Brightner was going to do to his captives never got done. You can't have everything, I guess.

It's a funny feeling to have somebody so scared of you. No, not funny. It makes me sad. I know that Rose is just as scared of lots of other people, too, though probably the ideas she has of why she's scared are delusions, not memories of real horrors that she got caught up in with Gran and me. I'm only sorry that she didn't get something good out of it all.

In the park, they've fixed up Wollman rink again. The "inexplicable disappearance" of a crane they'd been using for the repairs made the papers. A street gang sent the cops a note claiming "credit" for having kidnapped the crane. Ho-ho.

On a more personal level, Mom and I have never spoken Brightner's name between us. I'm not sure she remembers him too well, actually. She has taken up with one of her authors, a guy who writes thrillers—as if we needed thrills around here!—and she seems pretty happy.

Me, I am delighted. If she wants normal, she should have it. As she said herself, lots of people seem to like it fine.

Actually, being back in the ordinary groove suits me. I think I've had about all I want of the wild world of sorcery and so on for some time. I never thought I would feel this way. I mean, I not only helped Gran, I did some magic *myself,* with Barb's mirror and the silver glove.

However, a little of that goes a long way, particularly when you don't have a lot of spare time to stand around admiring what you've done and basking in your own glory. Life, as they say, goes on.

And besides, suppose I had done it wrong?

Also, in spite of what I told Gran, I do have moments of seeing Mom's point of view about the family talent. Moments of doubt. And dreams, sometimes, of not being able to find the mirror at the crucial moment, or of seeing Mom or Gran folded in the arms of Kali instead of Ushah. Things like that.

Gran says don't worry, you can't expect to go through a siege like that one without some aftereffects. She seems to have a lot of confidence in me. This is a good thing, since my own confidence tends to sort of wobble out of focus when I consider that I might have failed, after all.

Gran says the mages of Sorcery Hall are grateful for our efforts, which apparently have helped them in their war with Brightner's employers. Sorcery Hall itself seems to be out of immediate danger, which is a relief. But we don't talk about that stuff a lot.

I think Gran has a pretty good idea of my own feelings about what we've all just come through. She's not pushing anything. She says she doesn't want to distract me from the plain old business of growing up, and that when I'm ready for another dose of magic, I'll know it.

I only hope she's still around when that happens. She is a lot more frail than she was, I think. She's living in a residential hotel not far from us, which is not great—she says she misses some of the services of life at the home—but the life in the streets around her seems to entertain and stimulate her. She hardly ever forgets what's going on, so shortcake remarks are at a minimum.

I see her much more than I did when she was in New Jersey. She's teaching me to read Tarot cards, for the discipline, she says.

I said, "How come when you read my cards that day at the flea market, you couldn't see what was coming and warn me?"

Gran said, "The cards don't tell the future, you know. Nothing and no one can do that, since you create your future as you go along by the decisions you make. The cards showed what was *likely*, that was all. As it happened, the card called The Tower, which you said looked awful, turned out to be not quite what it seemed. It wasn't that you suffered disaster so much as that you were part of a disaster that another brought upon himself. Which I think you'll agree was not, in the long run, a bad thing."

Aside from some arguments about my learning the cards, and other more usual-type arguments, Mom and I are getting along better. Whenever I look at her I remember that I am the braver one, just as Gran said—at least as far as magic is concerned. And that gives me a strange, tender feeling about Mom. Love, probably. Just love.

Though she can be very annoying, of course. I mean, she is my *mom*, if you know what I mean. She still erupts when I forget to do things she's asked me to do, or when I tie up the phone, as if it were the end of the world, for cripes' sake. But she's better than she was about some things.

Yesterday the phone rang and I got to it ahead of her. I was expecting a call from Lennie, so naturally I answered, "Slime-coated Men; what can we do for you?"

Mom groaned and squinched up her eyes. "Oh, no, not Lennie again!" Then she thought a minute and added quietly, "Oh, well, I suppose there are worse faults than having one continuous eyebrow."

ABOUT THE AUTHOR

SUZY MCKEE CHARNAS is a well-known writer of fantasy and science fiction. Her other titles include *The Bronze King* and *The Golden Thread,* the other two books in the Sorcery Hall trilogy, as well as *Walk to the End of the World, Motherlines, Dorothea Dreams, The Vampire Tapestry,* and her novella "The Unicorn Tapestry," which won a Nebula Award in 1980. She lives with her husband in Albuquerque, New Mexico.